Tales from Darcy's Garden

Jan Dayton

Tales from Darcy's Garden

Volume 1
The Guardians
of the
Stickety Wicket Woods

XULON PRESS

Xulon Press
2301 Lucien Way #415
Maitland, FL 32751
407.339.4217
www.xulonpress.com

© 2019 by Jan Dayton

All rights reserved solely by the author. The author guarantees all contents are original and do not infringe upon the legal rights of any other person or work. No part of this book may be reproduced in any form without the permission of the author. The views expressed in this book are not necessarily those of the publisher.

Printed in the United States of America.

ISBN-13: 978-1-5456-7464-2

THIS BOOK IS DEDICATED TO

...Al, my husband and closest companion. Thank you for walking beside me through my challenges and frustrations. Thank you for never doubting my abilities. I am grateful for our early morning coffee dates. I appreciate the joy and laughter, the heartache and tears, the good times and bad times, and everything in between. I enjoy sharing my life with you. Thank you for your steadfast love, support, patience and your prayers.

To Mike, my loving son and *bright-light* of encouragement and joy. I am grateful for your love, friendship, your generous spirit and prayer support. Thank you for spurring me on with, "You can do this mom, I've got faith in you, and I'm very proud of you." Your tender heart and merry spirit are medicine for my soul. Keep on the path of *light and truth*.

...Annie, my precious pup, whose unconditional warm and fuzzy love, blesses my heart more than I can express. Her courage and determination to enjoy life, continually inspires me. Watching her navigate through life in total blindness, gives me understanding of what it means to "walk by faith, not by sight." She teaches me to "live in the moment" and enjoy the simpler things. She is my angel with fur.

My heart overflows with gratitude and love for our heavenly Father. He is my source of strength, faith, courage, and perseverance, enabling me to be a resilient overcomer. I thank Him for: His unfailing love, His blessings and gifts, and the privilege of allowing me to share the stories He gives me.

Chapter 1

Holy-Hocks and Hydrangel

In an ancient forest, known as the Stickety Wicket Woods, two sweet little fairies, Holy-Hocks and Hydrangel, are having a frolicking good time as they leap from blade to stone. They dance and giggle their way all along the thick, mossy path which will lead them all the way through the forest to the entrance of Marion's Meadow. They can't actually fly this early in the dawn of morning because their tiny, butterfly shaped wings, are heavy and wet from all the dazzling dew drops they encounter along the way. The two fairies have to stop now and then to flutter their wings and shake off the heavy dewdrops. Once they reach the meadow, the warm sun will dry their wings.

Today will be a very special day for Holy-Hocks and Hydrangel. A joyful fluttering is beating in their wee little hearts, making their Heart-Lights flicker much brighter than they had in a very long time. Ever since that dark day when they had arrived at the Stickety Wicket Woods, their brilliantly bright Heart-Light glows had been growing dimmer with the passing of so much time.

A gloomy cloud had come to this beautiful old forest, and it hovers over the two fairies at times, making them quite moody and cranky.

Instead of their usual merrymakings, this grey cloud sometimes causes them to play annoying pranks on others, or speak hurtful words to their closest and dearest forest friends. They are becoming increasingly frail and weak, and they are losing their most cherished and highly esteemed enchantment powers from Evermore. This made them very sad, especially on gloomy and cloudy days.

But alas, on this beautiful warm and sunny day, hope is in the air. Their Heart-Lights flickered with excitement. They sensed something was up. Whatever it was that was up, sure as the world, Holy-Hocks and Hydrangel felt certain that something good was going to happen for them today.

The Stickety Wicket Woods is located in the center of the Dale of Derby. It is a beautifully dense and ancient forest full of enchanting woodland wonders. This is where the forest folk and woodland critters live, in the cozy comfort of its seclusion and security. There are lots of woodsy dens, and snuggly, mossy hide-outs to keep the *wee* folks and critters hidden from the bad things. Most forest folk don't want anyone to know they are here, so they tuck themselves away, even when they aren't frightened. As far as Holy-Hocks and Hydrangel know, they are the only fairies living in the forest. The forest folk used to refer to them as the Bright-Light guardians of this woodland wonderland. Lately, the folks weren't sure that this was true anymore. When the Heart-Lights had started to dim, everyone in the forest knew that things were going to change, and not for the better.

Unbeknownst to Holy-Hocks and Hydrangel, there are lots of other *wee* folks in the forest, they have just been excellent at hiding. They often wonder if there are others like them living in the woods. Often, they had heard soft whisperings, and they even remembered being with others, but that was many years ago. Now that so much time has passed, most of those memories have faded. All they have left now are dreams of being in *another place at another time*. Holy-Hocks and Hydrangel are extraordinary fairies and *guardians* of the Stickety Wicket Woods.

Holy-hocks And Hydrangel

Holy-Hocks and Hydrangel adore all the woodland critters, including the Swampers who live in this enchanting forest. They are especially fond of the deer, fluffy bunnies, snow squirrels, soft grey mice, and little Brown Mouse. The fairies adore winged beings and among their favorites are the songbirds, butterflies, dragonflies, and red lady-bugs. Their furry and feathered friends are soft and warm to cuddle up to during the chillier days and evenings. They even love the slimy Swampers and find them friendly, playful, and most interesting to watch. Most of the residents of the Stickety Wicket Woods get along nicely, and they are good neighbors.

Just outside the forest, fluttering butterflies gather wildflower pollens in Marion's Meadow, a beautiful meadowland in the Dale of Derby. The meadowland surrounds the forest, and leads all the way from the Mountain of Mist on the north side of the Dale, to the Village of Dabney, and Darcy's garden.

As enchanting as the Stickety Wicket Woods may be, deep within its center, there is a dankly dark and misty place, called the Swamp. This is where all the slimy Swampers live. There are dozens of friendly green frogs and pudgy, warty toads. There are hundreds of wiggle and squiggle worms, slippery salamanders, and even a family of slow-moving and sloppy slugs. This swampy paradise is also home to some icky crit-ters of ill repute.

Smack dab in the middle of this swampland lies a scummy, limey-green pond full of stinky, mucousy goo. Folks from the Village of Dabney called this smelly water-hole "Skanky Pond." The Swampers enjoy living in their swampland home, but they never venture too close to that nasty pond. There are plenty of crystal-clear and clean creeks, and lots of fun and muddy puddles on the outermost edges of the Swamp. This is where they play, bathe, and drink. The forest folks, fairies, and all the woodland critters know to stay away from Skanky Pond. There are warning signs posted all over.

Rumor has it that a dragon-like monster lives way down deep within the gooey, limey-green waters of this disgusting pool of stench. For years, many scary stories have been told about this yucky pond monster and his foul gang of pond-scum goops. These creepy, icky things proudly call themselves "the Skankster Gang." They are stinky *slime-bags*. They've been known to slither out of the scummy waters to terrorize the little forest folk, the woodland critters, and especially the Swampers.

The Skanksters have even ventured into the Dale of Derby and the Village of Dabney to perform their hateful deeds. Their fearless leader, Marskank, the Darkled Dragon, never leaves the depths of his pond. Everyone hopes and prays he never does. He will slither up to the surface now and then to catch a breath of air, or to snatch a tasty morsel— usually a Swamper. On nights of the full moon, Marskank lets out eerie, growling howls. This howl, makes the forest critter's fur and feathers stand straight up, and chases them into the safety of their woodsy hide-outs. Misty fogs carry a foul-smelling swamp cloud through the forest, and often beyond. Marskank is confined to this murky prison ... at least for now.

From time to time, the village folks will catch a whiff or two of the foggy, grey swamp cloud, but only when the breezes blow in the right direction. The growling howls however, can be heard in the village no matter which way the winds blow. They know it's the Darkled Dragon who is doing the howling. This is not a sound anyone should ever have to hear. It will run chills down your spine and even make your skin crawl (meaning it feels as if a million bugs are crawling all over your body). It's a very creepy feeling indeed.

This is why warning signs have been posted at each entrance to the woods, all along the forest paths, and especially near the clearing that leads into the Swamp. The warning signs all read the same:

WARNING
STAY AWAY
FROM
SKANKY POND

Holy-hocks And Hydrangel

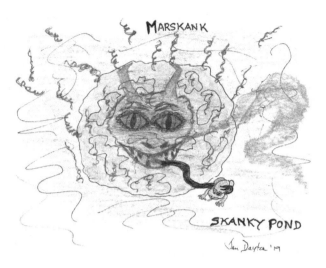

It's a good thing all the forest folks can read. In fact, not only are they smart enough to read, they are also smart enough to know when and where to hide. Whenever a Skankster creep slithers out of Skanky Pond, searching for innocent critters to terrorize, the forest has provided some nifty safety zones. Thank goodness this doesn't happen too often, but it happens often enough to keep everyone alert and always on the look-out.

When Holy-Hocks and Hydrangel became guardians of this wonderful forest, their bright glowing Heart-Lights had enabled them to do *search and rescues*. They could seek and find a missing critter, and scare off a Skankster, before any serious harm was done. However, their bright Heart-Light glows have dimmed over time. Something good needs to happen, and it needs to happen sooner ... not later.

Perhaps today?

Chapter 2

Tea Time in Darcy's Garden

Nearly every morning during late spring and summer, Holy-Hocks and Hydrangel gather fresh and tasty wild berries, from the berry patch in the meadow. They carry these colorful berries in little baskets across Marion's Meadow to Darcy's garden, following their *Fairy-Trail* path. They love to visit Darcy, and spend many days in her delightful garden. Darcy adores her two precious fairy friends, and they love her as well. They keep watch over her and have always protected her from any peril. However, they are weaker now, so it is difficult keeping Darcy and her pets, and other critters, safe from harmful intentions of dastardly menacers. Not only are the two fairies guardians of the forest, but they are also fierce protectors of Darcy's garden. They hope to continue protecting the peace, love, and joy within this beautiful garden, but they are going to need help.

Darcy's garden has always been a delightful place of goodness and merrymakings. It has also been a safe refuge for the two fairies and all of their woodland critter friends as well. They will continue their tea time garden visits as long as they have enough strength, to make it back and forth, across Marion's Meadow.

Tea Time In Darcy's Garden

Darcy always looks forward to spending time with Holy-Hocks and Hydrangel and their woodland critter friends, who often tag along. She loves serving the fairies their favorite *Fairy-time* teas and cookies and fresh wild berry scones. It's always warm and sunny in Darcy's garden in the spring and summer, and early autumn. Darcy grows the finest edible herbs and flowers, which are used to flavor the teas, cookies, and other sweets and savories. She also grows beautiful fragrant and colorful, flowers, which she puts in pretty vases on top of the tea tables.

This long-awaited day has finally arrived. Holy-Hocks and Hydrangel are beside themselves with anticipation. They don't know it yet, but Darcy has planned a royal tea party in their honor, for later this afternoon. Today is the day the royal prince of Evermore is bringing his divine gifts to present to the fairies. These gifts will be powerful blessings for each of them.

Darcy can hardly wait. She knows the fairies are expecting something wonderful to happen today, but just exactly what that something is has remained a well-guarded secret—hopefully.

Only a few trusted friends know about this surprise party and royal guest, and they had all promised to keep Darcy's secret. Surely they won't betray this kindhearted little girl's trust, will they? What if one of her friends lets the secret out? What will happen if a menacer hears about it? Darcy can't think about that right now. Since today is so full of goodness, even the tiniest bit of a *worriment* would be a terrible waste of a precious, happy time.

Many of the preparations are yet to be completed. Everything must be presented flawlessly and at just the right time. Darcy, her Mum, Ruthie, and her Aunt Jenny have carefully selected the tastiest teas, foods, and proper table settings for the 4 pm royal tea party. Several guests will probably arrive early to assure their places at the tables, even though all the seats have been reserved, for those who had answered the invitations.

On this special day of all days, Darcy has put extra fancy seeds in each of the decorative bird feeders throughout her garden. She has laid out fresh green lettuce and crunchy carrots for the fluffy bunnies. She even put out a nice tray of tasty cheeses for the soft grey mice, and for little Brown Mouse as well. Her beautiful and happy puppy, Annabelle, and her Aunt's very snooty and mouthy kitty, Clover, have been playing with all the forest critters since they had arrived with the fairies earlier this morning.

All the Sing-Song Birdies are practicing their glorious tunes. Shimmering butterflies, including the tiny yellow butterflies, are fluttering throughout the beautiful flowers. Dragonflies are dipping and darting about, while red ladybugs are hovering around the garden, on this beautiful, warm, and sunny morning. Honey bees have made their delicious wildflower honey, which will be served later today at the royal tea party. Joy and excitement fill the warm, fragrant springtime air.

Darcy is delighted to be hosting the royal tea party for her two, sweet fairy friends. Though only twelve years old, she has been taught the tea-time traditions from her mother and her aunt, since she had turned six.

In Darcy's garden, there are beautiful white benches. There is a sparkly little water pond, bird baths, a fountain, a garden swing, and pretty little tea tables. Victorian roses climb on white trellises and the garden gazebo. The fragrant roses display their beauty in soft artistic brushstrokes of deep reds, soft pinks, and lemony yellows. Purple falls of wisteria wind and twist their tender, grape-like vines, making beautiful, wispy wreaths and swags throughout the mazes of white wooden arches and arbors. A white picket fence surrounds the entire garden, behind the home where Darcy lives. A white picket entry gate welcomes all visitors to this delightful garden setting.

Edible herbs are growing strong in one of the corners of the garden. They are used for cooking, adding their flavors to many meals. Rosemary, lavender, and lemon-thyme herbs are often used to make the yummy *Fairy-Time* cookies. Several varieties of mints—including the preferred flavors of chocolate, orange, cinnamon, and spearmint—are spreading their tasty leaves on succulent stems. These tasty mint leaves can be used when brewing, adding fun flavors for Darcy's *Fairy-Time* teas.

Multitudes of flowering shrubs, planted all along the garden's fence, display their colorful artwork on white-picket easels. Hydrangea bushes proudly show off their giant, puffy balls of bright whites, sky blues, cotton-candy pinks, and even beautiful raspberry pinks. Blue lupines, sunny daffodils, multiple colors of bearded irises, and rosy-red tulips sway in ballet movements, flowing in rhythm with the warm, gentle springtime breezes. Waves of rainbow colors splash along the shorelines of the garden's flower beds. Brightly colored flowers will fill the pretty table-top vases and add their fragrant, floral beauty and elegance to the royal tea party.

For tea times, Darcy covers each table with delicate linens and lace. She uses her prettiest porcelain tea-cups, saucers, and matching dessert plates. She also uses her antique creamer and sugar set with a sterling silver sugar spoon. She likes to fill the sugar bowl with colorful rainbow sugar crystals, a favorite of the fairies and her other friends as well.

Later today, for the royal tea party, Darcy will be using her Grandmother's Tea set. It is covered with hand-painted pink roses and trimmed in gold. The set includes matching plates, cups and saucers, sugar bowl, creamer, and teapot. Ruthie is happy to let Darcy use these special items for the afternoon's festive event. This set will be used on the Royal Table.

For this morning's tea time, Darcy has filled her sugar bowl with the rainbow sugar crystals. Ruthie filled Darcy's creamer with the rich, fresh milk she drew from Bess, her dainty, black and white milk cow. Darcy loves it when her mother and aunt attend her *fairy-time* tea parties and the two women love playing *tea mums* and pouring the teas.

Since today's afternoon royal tea party is going to be extra special, Ruthie and Aunt Jenny will be helping Darcy with all the final preparations.

Darcy has collected a few tea-pots over the years, with the help and guidance from her aunt. Her favorite teapot is a special gift which Aunt

Jenny had brought back from London. She gave it to her niece on the day of Darcy's sixth birthday. This rare teapot is shaped like a merry-go-round with beautiful, hand-painted carousel ponies all around it. Aunt Jenny knows how much Darcy loves merry-go-rounds and carousel ponies, and she had hoped this gift would inspire her niece to want to learn about tea times. It most certainly did.

On this splendid and sunny, first day of May, the royal tea party, will begin promptly at 4 pm. Fancy handwritten invitations had been wax-sealed and sent several days ago.

The surprise guest, the Royal Prince of Evermore, Lord Ganador, is coming for sure. He will be traveling from his far-away kingdom.

Many of the fine folks from the Village of Dabney have been invited, and they will be attending. Several members of Darcy's family are also able to attend. Everyone is looking forward to this afternoon's special event.

Right now, it is mid-morning tea time, sometimes called "elevensies." Mum and Aunt Jenny are in the kitchen preparing the meats, vegetables, and fruits which will be served later today. They will be busy for a few hours. The Village Bakery, owned by the Pudding family, will be bringing fresh-baked goodies, including their famous decadent desserts. The Baker's Dozen, members of the Pudding family, will be arriving before the party to set up the food-serving tables. They will also be serving the guests.

The garden air is filling with melodious sounds of Bird-Song, and all the critters are happily playing. The little grey mice are dancing a jig, and little Brown Mouse is scratching his ears and tapping his feet to the rhythm of the music of the birds. Mrs. Buttupski and her two baby bunnies, Crunch and Rosebutt, are chomping on the crunchy carrots, and fresh green lettuce. Mrs. Buttupski and her frisky friend, little Brown Mouse, have just finished discussing plans for their next adventurous journey.

Tea Time In Darcy's Garden

Holy-Hocks and Hydrangel are sipping their mid-morning cinnamon mint tea and eating wild-berry scones with Devonshire cream. Aunt Jenny had just baked the scones, so they were fresh and warm. The scones were made with the fresh berries the two fairies had gathered in the meadow, bright and early this morning.

Darcy is reading a story to her friends from her book, *Tea-Time Tales and Fairytales*. This is a fun little book, which she herself has written. She is known throughout the village for her story-telling. Her school friends, Robin and Charlotte, along with her two fairy friends and critters love hearing her fun stories while sipping their tea and eating cookies and scones in this delightful garden.

Right now all is well in Darcy's garden and hopefully everything will go perfectly later this afternoon.

The royal prince has left Evermore and he is on his way.

Shh. Please!

Remember, Holy-Hocks and Hydrangel have no clue about this afternoon's royal tea party, or the invited prince.

For Holy-Hocks and Hydrangel, this afternoon's royal tea party and surprise visit from the Prince of Evermore, are going to make this "Day of All Days" a most memorable day indeed.

Chapter 3

Royal Preparations

Soon after the mid-morning tea time was over, the critters and fairies snuggled into their favorite garden places for nap time. Holy-Hocks has nestled herself into the bright pink Hollyhock blossoms growing on their tall leafy stalks. Hydrangel is all tucked up, inside a giant sky-blue Hydrangea puff. Pretty soon, sounds of soft, snoring poofs can be heard within Darcy's garden. The bright sun dazzles its glory, while fragrant springtime breezes whisper their way through Marion's Meadow, softly brushing over the tree tops of the Stickety Wicket Woods, gently flowing upwards to the top of the Mountain of Mist and Shimmer Lake.

Preparations begin.

On the western side of the Dale of Derby, a huge commotion is taking place inside the Bartletts' horse barn and royal stables. The majestic Pizzan horses are restless and all worked up. Blowing horse snorts and high-pitched whinnies, blast their way through the stables. Anxious horses, stomping in their stalls, make loud, clopping drum-beats with their hooves. Their excitement cannot be contained. Hired stable hands are bustling about, cleaning the barn from top to bottom. They

Royal Preparations

are scrubbing down each stall, and stacking newly-mowed hay bales. Fresh grain and oats have just been harvested and delivered to the barn.

A highly respected professional groomsman, Peter Rolph, and two of his aides are tending to the meticulous bathing and grooming of Blaze and Glory, two pure white Pizzan stallions. They had been gifted to the Bartlett family by Prince Ganador of Evermore. He had chosen to give these fine stallions to the Bartlett family, because of their pure royal bloodlines.

Blaze and Glory are the first-born twin sons of Prince Ganador's horse, Purity. Their magnificent beauty and unmatched strength make these two horses the only ones qualified to pull the Royal Gala Coach. Blaze and Glory's manes and tails are painstakingly rubbed with a special shining oil, and then combed and braided with royal purple and gold satin ribbons. Their long white manes and tails dazzle like full-moon shimmery reflections on a crystal-clear lake.

Blaze and Glory, the two twin stallions, simply can't be still. They are carrying their heads and tails high and proud, as they prance and dance around the stables. They are beyond excited. They understand the importance of their meticulous five-hour grooming by Peter and his aides. They will be pulling the Gala Coach with its royal passenger. They know they are going to see their father, Purity, very soon. It has been a very long time, and they have greatly missed him. It's no wonder they are so excited. Once Blaze and Glory have been fully groomed and dressed up, they will be harnessed and hooked up to the magnificent Royal Gala Coach.

The Royal Gala Coach has been getting a complete detailing. Nothing can be missed or left undone. The gold and white coach must be cleaned until it shines and sparkles like twinkling stars in a clear evening sky. The plush royal-purple velvet seat has to be carefully and thoroughly brushed clean. Every exquisite gold adornment on the exterior will be polished until it shines as bright as the noonday sun. Mr. Bartlett's son, James, will be driving, once the horses are harnessed and hooked to the prepared coach. James will wear his long-tailed red silk coat, black silk pants, and high-top hat. His riding boots will be polished to a mirrored, shiny black finish. Everything must be at its very sparkling best.

The royal stall is the largest and most important stall. It is located at the far end of the stables. It is being spotlessly cleaned and prepared for the prince's horse, Purity. Royal barn hands have been assigned to this duty, and they have cleaned and polished the pure gold, stall walls. The brilliant gold walls lit up the whole barn with a rich, warm, golden glow. The royal stall's floor has been scraped clean, properly washed, and freshly limed. Clean shavings have been spread ten to twelve inches thick, and the aroma of fresh cedar shavings fills the whole barn. The stainless-steel water trough and hay bin have been thoroughly disinfected and brightly polished.

It's very important that Purity's stall is meticulously cleaned, for he is by far the most excellent horse to ever bless the Bartletts' barn. This mighty horse is no ordinary horse. No, the horse belonging to the Royal Prince, Lord Ganador, is unlike any other horse known to mankind. Purity is a proud white stallion with absolutely no spots or blemishes of any kind. His master, Lord Ganador, is the royal guest who is coming to Darcy's garden later today. This explains all the *kerfuffle* in the Bartletts' barn.

Purity is a very special horse. He will be carrying the royal prince all the way from Evermore to Shimmer Lake, which lies at the top of the Mountain of Mist. This glorious mountain is located at the northernmost edge of the Dale of Derby, on the far side of the Stickety Wicket Woods, and just past Stones Throw.

Evermore, where Purity and Prince Ganador are coming from, is a faraway place from the world where Darcy and the fairies live. Some folks, including the wee folks and fairies, have heard of Evermore and its Prince, through various tales and stories, which have been passed down through the ages. According to some of these stories, Evermore exists in a faraway world in the great unknowns of the "Way Out There Somewhere." All anyone—wee folks or other folks—understands is that Evermore is so far away, that no living soul has ever seen this beautiful

Royal Preparations

place of glory. Holy-Hocks and Hydrangel, have mentioned that they remembered something like it, in one of their "Another Place at Another Time" dreams.

It's a real *wonderment* how the heck Purity will get himself and the Prince, all the way from Evermore to the top of the Mountain of Mist, and then to Darcy's garden by 4 pm today. But, Purity is no ordinary horse. He flies, with two large and very beautiful wings. They are something like the feathery wings of birds and angels, but they are far more powerful.

There is a huge difference between Purity's wings and any other wings. Many of his brilliant white feathers are glittered with sparkling silver-dust. The larger feather quills are filled with 100 percent pure liquid gold. It is the liquid gold that produces all the power. When the sun shines on these magnificent wings just right, you can actually see bolts of lightning flashing through them. Purity's wings are like no other, and marvelous to behold.

Purity loves flying Lord Ganador through the puffy white clouds and bright blue skies throughout all of the "Way Out There" heavens. The Prince and his horse also enjoy taking midnight rides through the winking and twinkling stars of crisp, clear nighttime skies. As powerful as this gallant steed is, Purity is also a very gentle and kind horse. He willingly yields his strength to his master, and he is always available and pleased to take Lord Ganador on each and every assigned journey, no matter where. Today's assignment is no exception.

Today, the royal prince has a very special event to attend, later this afternoon, and so Purity has been summoned. As soon as Purity hears his master's whistle, he is there in a *flash*, ready for the journey. He will bring Lord Ganador to meet the Royal Gala Coach, at the base of the Mountain of Mist. But first, they will land on top of the mountain and rest near the beautiful lake there. As soon as they make landing, Purity will take a refreshing drink from the crystal clear and frosty waters of Shimmer Lake. The Prince will rest a bit in the cool, soft and green grasses beside the sparkling, living waters of the lake. There, Lord

Ganador will renew his strength for the rest of the trip downward, to the base of the mountain.

The kingdom of Evermore is very far away, and this journey is extremely important. Therefore, prince and horse must make it in record-breaking time. That is why they will both take this brief, but much needed, time of rest. Once rested, they will continue to the base of the Mountain of Mist. There, the Royal Gala Coach will be ready, and waiting, to take Lord Ganador to Darcy's garden for the royal tea party.

As soon as Lord Ganador and Purity reach the base of the mountain, Purity will be handed over to Peter Rolph, and his assistants.

Peter and his aides will quietly lead Purity to his private royal stall in the Bartletts' barn. There he will be well fed and groomed. His wings will be carefully dusted with a special tool called a wing-feathers duster. Purity will then rest quietly and wait for his master Prince to summon him, for their return trip home to Evermore.

It has been a very tedious day for all the Bartletts' stable hands, groomsmen, and driver, James. The Royal Gala Coach is prepared and ready. Blaze and Glory are all dressed out and harnessed. James and Peter are hooking them to the coach. They will be leaving in a few moments. The coach will arrive on time to pick up the royal prince.

Lord Ganador and Purity have completed their much-needed rest at the top of the Mountain of Mist and Shimmer Lake. It is time for the prince to mount his horse and head down to the base of the mountain.

It looks like their timing is perfect.

The Royal Gala Coach and its driver, James, will be arriving at the base of the Mountain of Mist at the perfect time. Peter Rolph and his aides will be there as well, ready and waiting to tend to Purity.

Purity will have just the right amount of time to enjoy a delightful visit with his twin sons, Blaze and Glory, before Peter Rolph and his aides have to lead him to the royal stall in the Bartletts' barn.

It won't be long now, before Lord Ganador arrives at Darcy's garden for the 4 pm Royal Tea Party. His timing is always perfect, so he will arrive at exactly the right time.

Chapter 4

The Royal Tea Party and Surprise Guest

Meanwhile, in Darcy's garden, mid-morning tea is over and the fairies and critters are still napping. Darcy, her mum Ruthie, and Aunt Jenny are scrambling around, finishing the final preparations for this afternoon's royal tea party.

A crown pork roast has been cooking in the oven for a few hours. Several fresh herbs, and spices had been added to the roast for extra flavor. The kitchen smelled delicious, making mouths water. Aunt Jenny finishes chopping the veggies and begins seasoning them with fresh herbs. They will be roasted in the oven. Ruthie places freshly sliced veggies and tasty ripened fruits on beautiful platters to be chilled. Darcy is busy filling clear crystal bowls with the sweet wildflower honey.

The "Baker's Dozen Team" are coming from the Village Bakery, owned by the Pudding family. They are bringing freshly baked breads and beautiful decadent desserts. They will set up the food-serving tables, and properly display all the foods. The Baker's Dozen volunteered to serve the guests later today, and have offered to pour the teas as well. This is a relief for Darcy, her mum, and her aunt. Now, the three ladies can relax and enjoy the event with their guests. This extra help is greatly appreciated.

The tea tables are all set, and topped with colorful flowers in crystal vases. The fairies have their own table, right next to the royal tea table where Lord Ganador, Darcy, Ruthie and Aunt Jenny will be sitting. The Royal Table is extra special. It is covered with a fine, Irish lace cloth which hangs to the ground. Ribbons of purple and gold are tied in four bows and pinned to the tablecloth. The centerpiece is a beautiful crystal vase filled with fragrant, deep red Victorian roses and fresh-cut baby's breath. The roses smell delightful. Darcy is pleased and proud. She purposely placed Holy-Hocks and Hydrangel's table and chairs on a stand right next to where she will be sitting, so she can cut the fairies' food into tiny, crumb-like pieces. Final inspections are done. Everything is perfectly beautiful.

The Baker's Dozen from the Village Bakery have just arrived. They are busy setting up the food-serving tables. The party guests will be arriving shortly.

It's time to bathe and dress up for the royal tea party.

Darcy had awakened Holy-Hocks and Hydrangel, and she asked them to bathe, dress, and fix each other's hair real pretty. She gave them brand new fancy dresses to put on. She had just told them about the royal tea party, but not about the surprise guest, or that this party is being held in their honor. They jumped up and down and fluttered, all excited.

Holy-Hocks and Hydrangel rush over to the sparkly little pond, do a quick splash bath, and wash and dry their hair. They put on their fancy new dresses. As a final touch, they tie fresh flowers together and weave them into each other's hair. They look absolutely beautiful. They can hardly believe that they are going to be attending a *royal tea party*. They have just seen all the fancy tea tables, and they are feeling very "special" right now. They had been sensing that *something good* was going to happen for them today. Could this special tea party be it?

The Royal Tea Party And Surprise Guest

Darcy had informed the fairies that several of the village folks will be coming, as well as many of her family members. The fairies know how to behave properly, but Darcy is still a bit nervous and she had warned them, "No *fairy-funny business.*" They promised to be on their best behavior, but then they started thinking about the decadent desserts. Now they are getting fidgety. Regular food is OK, but not nearly as good as chocolatey, decadent desserts, wildflower honey, and rainbow sugar. They have what is called the "sweet tooth," and both of them have it really bad.

Darcy finishes dressing herself, and she is looking really sweet and pretty in her long, white, sleeveless sundress. It has lace flowers trimming the neck and hemline. There is a soft pink satin cummerbund and a pink hair bow to match. Ruthie brushes her daughter's shiny, golden brown hair and attaches the pretty pink bow to the back of her head. She looks absolutely adorable. She is a precious little girl with a tender heart and many gifts. Darcy puts on her dressy white shoes to complete her outfit. She is ready.

Ruthie and Aunt Jenny are wearing long, colorful, floral sun dresses, floppy sun hats to match, and white gloves. Hats and white gloves are a must for the ladies. At twelve, Darcy has a choice, and she has chosen not to wear either a hat or gloves. Her pretty pink hair-bow will be proper enough, and white gloves will only get dirty while she's cutting up the food for the fairies.

Holy-Hocks and Hydrangel show up to Darcy's table. They look so cute, all dressed up in their fancy little sun dresses. Aunt Jenny had made the special dresses for each of them. Holy-Hock's dress is lavender and Hydrangel's dress is blue. They had woven pretty wild-flowers into each other's hair. Darcy takes one look at them, and beams with pride. She scoops them up to hug them. The three of them giggle with pure delight.

It is now fifteen minutes to 4 pm, on this "Day of All Days."

The invited guests are arriving.

The first guests to arrive are Sir Carlton and Lady Dora-Lee Bartlett. They are family, and own the world-famous Pizzan horses. Their home, training barn, and stables are located in the hilly area on the western side of the Dale of Derby. You can see the Bartletts' barns from the park in the village. The Bartletts are Ruthie and Jenny's first cousins. Their son, James, won't be attending. He is driving the Royal Gala Coach, which is bringing the Royal Prince Lord Ganador to Darcy's garden, promptly at 4 pm.

The next guests to arrive are Mr. and Mrs. White, Dale and Caroline. They are also cousins, and they have travelled all the way from London for this special event. They are staying at the Gracious Goodness Manor, the beautiful Victorian inn just outside the village. This inn is located near the west entrance to the Village Market and Shoppes on Devonshire Street. The Whites are known the world over for their famous wooden, hand-carved, painted ponies. These are the beautiful carousel ponies you see on merry-go-rounds all over the world. The White family is a very wealthy bunch, but they are not snobby about their riches. They are very humble, generous, and kind. They had taken time out from their busy schedule, to attend Darcy's royal tea party. They adore the little girl, and are proud of her many gifts and talents.

Mr. and Mrs. Bo-Peep, Bill and Betty, show up shortly after the Whites, and are promptly seated next to the Bartletts. They are family as well, and own the sheep pastures to the northeast of the village, just on the other side of Marion's Meadow. From Darcy's garden, you can see their sheep grazing on the foothills all spring and summer, and most of the Autumn. During the coldest nights of wintertime, the sheep are kept in "sheep shacks," which are small, wooden, tin-roofed, shed-like buildings.

Darcy and the fairies are getting more and more excited watching the guests arrive and they can hardly wait to see who arrives next.

Darcy loves having all her family together, which is rare, due to the busyness of everyone's lives, and long distances some of them have to travel. She has a wonderful family. Her aunts, uncles and cousins always treat her kindly, giving her the happy childhood she deserves. They had heard many stories of Darcy's two fairy friends, but no one

The Royal Tea Party And Surprise Guest

had actually seen Holy-Hocks and Hydrangel. They all looked forward to meeting them.

Several of the village shop owners have arrived, including Darcy's Aunt Dottie. She is Ruthie's older sister, who owns the Tipsy Topper Hattery. The sisters had named the shop Tipsy Topper, because Aunt Dottie was known to like the taste of aged Wild-Berry juice, and whenever she drinks a wee-bit too much, Dottie gets a little tipsy. She's a very humorous little old lady, with a great gift of gab. All the village ladies love to visit her shop and try on her hand-made hats. If they're lucky enough, Dottie will offer them a glass of the aged juice, making the ladies tipsy as well. Lots of giggles and lots of happy ladies come out of that fun little hat shop.

Pastor Charles and his wife, Ima Rightwun, are from the Good Church in the village. They have arrived, and are seated next to the Whites. The Good Church, for the folks of the faith, sits across the street from Darcy's house. Darcy, Ruthie, and Aunt Jenny never have to go very far to hear Pastor Charles speak the Good News, from the Good Book at his pulpit, inside the quaint little church. Ima Rightwun is the Sunday School teacher. She does a good job teaching the village kids the right way to live from the Good Book stories. Right or wrong, kids will be kids, right? She also teaches K-12 in the one-room schoolhouse, which is attached to the back of the church. Prayer and other important meetings are held there as well.

It is now 4 pm: party time.

The Royal Gala Coach is pulling up. The driver, James, shouts "Whoa!" Blaze and Glory immediately stop. James steps down, just as the Village Ding-Dong Bell Tower dings its fourth dong. James helps Lord Ganador out of the coach and walks him to the garden gate, where one of the Baker's Dozen greets him with a bow, and leads him to the royal table. He announces the prince. Everyone stands and bows. James drives away.

Holy-Hocks and Hydrangel are astonished, and ask themselves, "Who is this handsome young man, and why does he have a gold crown on top of his head? Why is he wearing a long purple coat, white pants, black high boots, and pure white gloves? White gloves? Really? Of all things."

Then, Holy-Hocks and Hydrangel start whispering to each other, "Sure hope he takes those white gloves off, before he eats his dessert, and gets them all chocolatey and sticky-dirty." They just can't help themselves. The "giggle fits" take over. They are immediately embarrassed, as Darcy gives them one of those "Looks" just like a mother will, when her child giggles, burps, or worse, *poots* at the wrong time in the right place, like church. Yikes! This is all a little too much fussiness for the fairies, and with Darcy's glaring *look,* they know they need to try to control themselves. They finally manage to stand up and bow to the Prince. It's really more of a curtsy because of their tiny size.

Music in the Air

With the arrival of the first guests, the Sing-Song Birdies had started their repertoire of songs. It now sounds like there is a fiddle and a tambourine playing with the Sing-Song Birdie band. Everybody figures it must be the mockingbirds, since they are able to mimic all kinds of sounds. However, it is actually Twinx and Taloop, two other fairies who nobody knows about.

Twinx is playing a Fiddle while Taloop is shaking a tambourine, keeping time with the Bird-Song. They had been hiding in the rose bushes all afternoon. Nobody knew they were there. Holy-Hocks and Hydrangel hadn't seen them, and they didn't even know they existed. Unless, they had been in their dreams of "Another Place at Another Time"

Teas are poured, the food is served and everyone is enjoying the delicious and savory, main course meal. There is a lot of chatter going on at the tea tables, mostly compliments of how beautiful everything looks and how delicious the food tastes. Some folk's chatter is about other folks who aren't even there. They don't believe they are gossiping. They are just making conversation. They feel it's OK to talk about others, as long as they say nice things about them. Mostly this is true, but sometimes chattering about others *can* turn into gossip. To avoid gossip, remember this, "If you don't have anything nice to say about someone, don't say anything at all."

The music continues and some of the little critters are dancing with each other. Holy-Hocks and Hydrangel are fluttering their wings and arms in rhythm with the tambourine beats. What a fun time. This joyful music has put everyone in a very happy mood.

Darcy has cut the meat and veggies into tiny crumb-like morsels. She even pulled the breadcrumbs apart for Holy-Hocks and Hydrangel. They are pretending to enjoy this savory meal. However, impatience is getting in the way, and they start pestering Darcy for something sweet. They want their decadent desserts, and they want them right now!

The Sweet Tooth is raging. Hydrangel starts plotting and planning.

Hydrangel Takes A Decadent Leap

Without warning, impatient Hydrangel lifts herself off her chair, and flits directly toward the decadent dessert tables. Darcy watches this abomination of rudeness in absolute horror. Lord Ganador is watching Darcy, causing her to flush. She wonders how in the world Hydrangel can do such an improper thing. She thought she had taught the fairies better than this. She had, but Hydrangel's Sweet Tooth *will* have its own way.

Darcy turns her glare towards a worried and wide-eyed Holy-Hocks. Darcy gives her the *look*. You know, the *look* that speaks volumes, without saying a word. The *look* that says, "Don't even think about it!"

Holy-Hocks drops her head, tucks her chin to her chest, and waits for Darcy to move her glaring eyes elsewhere. She does. Darcy is back to focusing her eyes on Hydrangel. It seems this little *imp* has been gathering crumbs from a chocolatey caramel brownie. As best as she could, she had folded them into the skirt of her dress. Egads! Her white, lacy slip is showing, and it's covered with gooey chocolate smears. Oh, my! Poor Darcy is completely appalled, and her face is fully flushed now. The

Prince, Lord Ganador, has to stifle a little chuckle. So, he clears his throat and immediately turns his head to speak to Ruthie and Aunt Jenny.

Darcy stands up and politely says, "Excuse me, please." She heads toward the decadent dessert tables. She hopes and prays, that no one had seen this little misbehaved fairy with her hiked up skirt, her lacy, chocolatey, smeared slip, and worse.

Sticky crumbs from that chocolate caramel brownie are now spilling out of the folds of Hydrangel's skirt. She had poorly hidden her goods. Oh, my goodness, what a mess! Soon, the *little darling* is tripping over soft and gooey, caramel frosting, and sinking deeper into the chocolatey brownie delight. Just when Darcy thinks it can't get any worse, PLOP! There goes Hydrangel. She is now sitting, not on top of, but deep down in the middle of all this decadent goodness. She is up to her knees and butt in the sticky-gooey caramel frosting and rich chocolate brownie. Darcy quickly snatches Hydrangel up, and out of the brownie, which makes a sucking sound, as she pulls her out. Off to the kitchen Darcy rushes, with a very sticky, gooey, chocolatey, and messy, but happy Hydrangel.

Darcy pours warm water into a tea-cup, adds some dish soap, and dips Hydrangel into the sudsy water. As Darcy removes Hydrangel's dress, brownie crumbs and gooey caramel stickiness start flying all over the place, including the back wall behind the kitchen sink. And, don't you know, Hydrangel keeps licking her fingers and dipping them into the gooey crumbs as Darcy frantically tries to clean her up. Soon, chocolatey finger prints are showing up all over the place. Even Hydrangel's pudgy little face and puckered mouth are completely covered with chocolatey, fudgy caramel smudges. Darcy is pretty upset, and she thinks the clean-up is going to take more time than she had hoped. But, she's determined.

Phew! After a sudsy bath, and some rather stern words, Darcy puts a clean dress on Hydrangel. To Darcy, this ordeal seemed to have taken forever, but it had only taken fifteen minutes from the time she brought Hydrangel to the kitchen, got her cleaned up and re-dressed. They were finally ready to return to the party. Darcy was hoping that no one had noticed them missing, or why.

Darcy and Hydrangel make it back to the royal tea table, and they are acting as if nothing had ever happened. Nobody says a word to Darcy, nor do they even dare to look at her, or her little fairy friend.

However, this little mishap, had *not* gone unnoticed. Everyone had been watching Hydrangel's decadent dessert caper, and now they are having to stifle their little chippers of giggles. Hiding their grinning mouths behind the linen dinner napkins, the guests manage to cover their laughter with fake coughs and several throat clearings. Although these fine guests had found Hydrangel's misbehaving antics very funny and cute, no one could ever admit it, for that would not be proper at all.

So, everyone carries on as if nothing had ever happened. They continue eating and chatting with each other. Darcy finally calms down.

The fairies, however, are still impatiently waiting for their sugary decadent desserts. They begin tapping their feet and slapping their hands on their legs, under the table, wondering if they will ever get to enjoy their sweets.

The "Sweet Tooth" keeps on raging.

Finally, the best of all things happens. One of the Baker's Dozen is at Darcy's royal tea table, clearing the plates, while another rolls the two decadent dessert carts straight over to her table. Holy-Hocks and Hydrangel start jumping up and down, clapping their tiny hands with joy. Once again, they get the *look.* Both fairies immediately sit back down, fold their tiny little hands on their tiny little laps, and look up demurely at Darcy. Her heart melts with a warm, tender love for these two precious, though very precocious, tiny-winged beings. Darcy could never, ever, stay mad at them, not for very long anyway.

Chapter 5

Gifts and Blessings

After the royal tea party had ended, all the guests were full and happy. The meal had been delicious. The yummy, decadent desserts were enjoyed by all. Before the cleanup, Lord Ganador stood up, walked over to the garden gazebo, and stepped up to the podium. He turned around to face all the guests. He blew his whistle softly, to get everyone's attention. Pretty soon all the village guests, Darcy, her mother and aunts, their family, and all the critters gathered in front of the Gazebo.

Holy-Hocks and Hydrangel flitted over to their long-time best friend, Darcy. Several woodland critters were either sitting down or standing, all around and in between, many of the guests. Some of the smaller critters were sitting on some of the guest's shoulders, making it easier for them to see better. Sing-Song birdies were whistling, directing everyone into place. As soon as Lord Ganador had his captive audience, he spoke. He asked Holy-Hocks and Hydrangel to come up to the podium.

Mrs. Buttupski left her babies with little Brown Mouse, and hopped over to the two fairies, to offer them a ride to the gazebo. Once at the

Gifts And Blessings

gazebo, the prince bent down and tenderly gathered Holy-Hocks and Hydrangel into his hands. Mrs. Buttupski returned to her babies. Lord Ganador brought the two fairies before his face, and he held them so they were looking straight into his beautiful kind eyes. He looked gently into their eyes, for a few moments. As he did this, their Heart-Lights began to flicker. He seemed vaguely familiar to both of them. Then, he set them on top of the podium before him, and asked them to turn and face the audience. They immediately obeyed. All of a sudden, Holy-Hocks and Hydrangel both, remembered it all. Together, they turned back around and knelt before Lord Ganador, and wept. Instantly, they knew in their hearts that they had been with him before.

All those dreams they'd been having through the ages, those fading dreams of "Another Place, at Another Time," were coming back to them in short, lightning flashes of photo-like images.

Lord Ganador gently smiled at Holy-Hocks and Hydrangel. The guests and critters were astonished, and soon, noisy chattering stirred in the garden. "What was happening?" the guests asked each other. Confused, they all chattered at the same time. The Prince raised his arms and spoke one word, "Peace." The quiet sense of calm, immediately resumed its peaceful position in Darcy's garden. Not a sound, a peep, or even a chirp could be heard. As soon as Lord Ganador had spoken that word, everyone hushed. They know how important it is to be still, and listen, whenever the Prince of Evermore speaks.

He gently lifted the fairies back to their feet and asked them to bow their heads. They did. Then he reached into his right pocket and withdrew two, tiny, gold-wrapped gift boxes. Lord Ganador asked them both to step forward. They did. He opened both boxes and carefully pulled out two tiny gold necklaces. Beautiful, jeweled angel wings hung from shiny chains. He placed the necklaces around each of the fairy's tiny necks. Their Heart-Lights stopped flickering, and quickly brightened to a beautiful warm glow. Holy-Hocks and Hydrangel wept tears of joy. Lord Ganador put each tear-drop in tiny *Tear Bottles,* which he kept in his pocket.

Then the prince asked them both to turn around. As soon as they were facing the audience, he proclaimed these words over both of them, "These are my beloved angels." Next, he asked everyone in the audience to bow their heads. They did. Lord Ganador declared this blessing over Holy-Hocks and Hydrangel, "They were with me from the beginning, and they will be with me forever and ever, in my kingdom of Evermore."

He then asked everyone to face him again. They did. He called Darcy up to the gazebo. She stood before him as he took another gold-wrapped gift box out of his pocket. He opened it and withdrew a jeweled angel wings necklace just like the ones he had given to the fairies, only bigger. Darcy bowed her head as Lord Ganador put the wings necklace around her neck. He proclaimed this blessing over her: "You are My beloved child, and because you know and love me, you have a special place waiting for you, in Evermore."

Darcy gathered the two fairies from the podium, and walked back over to her mother. She held Holy-Hocks and Hydrangel in the palms of her hands.

Everyone waited to see what Lord Ganador was going to do next. He asked all the guests to bow their heads again. They did. Even the critters bowed their heads. He proclaimed his blessings of *peace and joy* over Darcy's garden. He blessed the Village of Dabney, Marion's Meadow, and the Living Waters Stream. He blessed the Bo-Peeps, their sheep and pastures. He blessed the Bartletts, and their beautiful horses. He blessed the Good Church, the schoolhouse, Pastor Charles, and his wife, Ima Rightwun. He blessed the Gracious Goodness Inn, and all of the guests staying there. He continued his blessings on all the wonderful folks and their pets, in this beautiful valley, known as the Dale of Derby. When he got to the Stickety Wicket Woods, he paused for a moment. When Lord Ganador was ready, he blessed the forest, swamp, and all the *good* little forest folks and critters who live there. He stopped again, and waited.

Then, Lord Ganador gave a stern warning. He told his audience that he'd heard the rumors of a monster, living in the depths of The Skanky Pond. The nasty, goopy pond in the center of the Stickety Wicket Woods

Gifts And Blessings

Swamp. He said most of the rumors were true. He knew all about that evil Darkled Dragon, "Marskank," and his gang of Skanksters, and Dim-Lits, who had arrived at the Ancient Forest many years ago.

Lord Ganador praised Holy-Hocks and Hydrangel, for restoring the ancient forest and saving the trees which had been slowly dying, since Marskank had arrived. He thanked them for guarding the enchanted forest and all its woodland critters. It had taken most of their "Bright-Light" strength to do so, and their Heart-Lights were dimming. He had heard Darcy's request, and he had chosen to come to her garden, today. He gave them the angel wings necklaces to restore their powers. He understood exactly why the two fairies had lost their Powers from Evermore.

Marskank had been at work.

Next, he made the following statement, "I will be coming back to find the lost ones, belonging to the tribe of Bright-Lights, from my kingdom. I hope to restore them to their former positions." He went on to explain that Holy-Hocks, Hydrangel, and other wee folks, just like them, had been with him in the realm of Evermore, ages ago. They had been majestic, angelic beings in his kingdom. Holy-Hocks and Hydrangel had been his anointed keepers of peace and hope. They had been anointed guardians over all the children, the animals, the forest and the meadowlands, in this valley. Plus, they were appointed as keepers of all the sparkling and living waters, and bountiful gardens, in this earthly valley, known as, the Dale of Derby.

Many of the Bright-Lights had gone missing from Evermore, and Lord Ganador was hoping to find them all. He asked all the guests in the audience to keep their eyes and ears open. He asked them to report any signs or sightings of the wee folks, who could be living anywhere in the Dale. He thought most of them were hiding in the Stickety Wicket Woods.

Right away, several of the guests started murmuring. One by one, they told the prince how they were pretty sure they'd seen some of the wee folks, or at least some evidence of their presence. Everybody promised to get a message to the prince as soon as they had any reliable information. They weren't quite sure how the heck they could get in touch with him, but later on they were going to find out how.

An Offer is Presented

Lord Ganador changed the subject. He said to the guests, "I have come this day to offer Holy-Hocks and Hydrangel, an opportunity." Then he spoke directly to the two fairies. He started to say to them, "My little ones, you can return with me to Evermore, tomorrow morning at first light—" Immediately, he was interrupted by Darcy's gasp. The little girl's heart churned in agony, as soon as the prince spoke these words. She had known these precious fairies ever since she was a very little girl, maybe even since she was a baby. Darcy fought the tears as best as she could, but a few betrayed her and fell down her reddening cheeks.

Instantly, Holy-Hocks and Hydrangel sensed Darcy's pain. They flickered up and down in her hands, trying to comfort her. They gathered each of her tears and offered them to Lord Ganador, which touched his heart. He took each of Darcy's tears from the fairies, and put them in another tears bottle. He blessed them, and tucked them into his pocket.

The kind Prince thought long and hard. He asked the fairies if they wanted to stay here with Darcy and all their forest friends, and go on just exactly as things had been for a long, long time. They could remain as fairies, and use their angel wings necklaces to call up the powers of Evermore, whenever they needed. If they chose to stay, their assignment would be to help others search for all the lost members of the Bright-Lights Tribe, and to defeat the members of the Darkled Dragon's Tribe.

To be fair, the Prince decided to continue explaining his first offer. If they chose to go home with him, he would hold a wings ceremony as soon as they arrived back in Evermore. They would be transformed back to the glorious angelic beings they had once been. They would resume their former positions, but they would receive new assignments. He gave them a few moments to decide.

Gifts And Blessings

With their memories mostly restored, they knew how wonderful it had been for them in Evermore. This was a painful decision for them, because they knew what it meant. It meant that Darcy wouldn't be able to see them anymore. They would be far, far away. No more tea times and fairy tales in Darcy's garden. No more wild-berry scones or rainbow sugar. No more wildflower honey, and no more chocolatey decadent desserts. No more fun rides on Mrs. Buttupski, and no more snuggles with their furry woodland friends. This was a heart-aching choice for them to make.

Darcy's heart was torn in two. She wanted to make their choice less painful, while her heart broke in pieces. This twelve-year-old little girl had already known the gut-wrenching pain of loss. Yet, her selfless love for Holy-Hocks and Hydrangel made her heart desire what would be best for them. Even if it meant saying goodbye to all the joy they had brought her, Darcy thought of them first. Putting aside her pain, she loved them enough to let them go. This was true love. Lord Ganador was watching Darcy.

Darcy knew in her heart of hearts that Holy-Hocks and Hydrangel had been created for something far greater than her little tea-parties and fairy tales.

They might be tiny fairies, but they had huge powerful heart-glows of pure love. The tender compassionate kind of love that had healed Darcy's heart and given her the strength and courage she needed, after her father had abandoned her and her mother. They were there for her when she lost her best friend, Loretta, to a horrible disease. They had even introduced her to her new best friend Robin, when he and his family moved into the Dale of Derby, a year ago. They were always there for her.

So, as heartbreaking as this was for Darcy, she still wanted nothing but the very best for her two precious fairy friends. They deserved it. When Lord Ganador saw Darcy's selfless, kind and compassionate heart, it tweaked his own gentle heart. These were his children and he loved them all. He needed more time to think. He would come up with the best idea, one that would work, and not cause a heartache for anyone. His time here was running short, so the decision was postponed.

Time to Go

The Royal Gala Coach will be arriving soon to pick up Lord Ganador and carry him to meet Purity at the base of the Mountain of Mist. He really needs to leave for Evermore, no later than tomorrow morning. Another urgent assignment is waiting for him there.

He grabbed Darcy, gave her a gentle hug, and as he wiped her tears, he told her not to worry. He would protect her heart, he promised. Then he took Holy-Hocks and Hydrangel from Darcy and held them in his white gloved hands. He brought them up to his face and smiled gently at their worried little expressions. He tenderly spoke these words: "Have no fear my little ones, for my love for you is good, and I will never harm you. I will be back another day, very soon. Meanwhile, you may stay here with your beloved Darcy and continue with your guardianship duties. But, you must help search for your lost friends of the Bright-Lights Tribe." They agreed.

Lord Ganador explained how to contact him. He told them, "You can contact me with your wings necklaces. They are pre-programmed. If you look at the back of the wings, you'll find two red buttons. Just push the red "O" button (for Operator) and leave any important messages on my special answering machine. I will get back to you as quick as I can."

In case of an immediate emergency, he told them to push the red "SOS" button (for HELP). Immediately, troops from Evermore will be sent down to help.

One very important thing Holy-Hocks, Hydrangel, and Darcy needed to understand. Lord Ganador spoke firmly. "*Do not* lose your wings necklaces. Never take them off. Guard them carefully." he warned. They understood.

He told the fairies that inside each gift box, there were instruction manuals, in case they forgot how to call up the Powers of Evermore. These instructions also explain which powers to use for every situation.

Gifts And Blessings

As he bid them all farewell, he thanked everyone for the beautiful royal tea party. He tipped his crown to Darcy and the fairies. They immediately bowed. Then, he walked to the gate and stepped out of the garden, just as James pulled up with the Gala Coach and Blaze and Glory.

Everyone waved goodbye. They watched as the coach drove off toward Marion's Meadow. Someone heard a growling howl.

The Ground Trembles.

The last of the guests were about to leave Darcy's garden, as a grey, misty cloud leeched its way through the trees along the edges of the Stickety Wicket Woods. It was heading into the meadow. There was a slight whiff of pungent air. The ground trembled and there was a loud crashing sound.

Screaming horse whinnies were heard, off in the distance. They came from the direction the Royal Gala Coach was headed. Something terrible was happening. As the guests and Darcy watched in horror, the ground near the woods seemed to open up. They caught sight of the Coach and the two horses, Blaze and Glory. Something was tossed off the coach, it must have been James, the driver. Then the horses and coach were swallowed up and disappeared into the ground.

Several of the men ran into Marion's Meadow to see what had happened, and to offer their help. Others went to find ropes and wagons. The rest of the guests stayed behind and watched, terrified. Villagers ran out of their homes and headed to where Darcy and the guests stood, in shock. Pastor Charles and Ima ran across the street to Darcy's to offer help and prayers.

What just happened!?

Chapter 6

The Crash

Right after the Gala Coach had picked up Lord Ganador, and the growling howl was heard, a small cloud of putrid air slithered its way toward Darcy's garden. Darcy quickly gathered Holy-Hocks, Hydrangel, and all their critter friends. She tucked them into their safety zones, in the garden. Aunt Jenny put Annabelle and Clover inside the house to keep them safe. She and Darcy returned to join the other folks who were watching in horror.

The Gala Coach had been taking Lord Ganador across Marion's Meadow to the other side of the forest. It was heading to the Mountain of Mist, where Lord Ganador was to meet his horse, Purity. Together, they were to make the long journey back home to Evermore at first light of morning. As they were crossing the meadowlands, a sink-hole opened on the far side of the meadow, and a deep ravine was exposed.

James heard a loud thundering sound, as the ground trembled beneath them. He wasn't able to see the hole opening up just ahead, in time. Just as they got close enough to see the hole, an icky black Skankster ran in front of Blaze and Glory, and spooked them. Both horses reared up on their hind legs. James lost control of the reins, and

The Crash

fell off the coach. The horses got tangled up in the loose reins and tumbled over the edge of the huge opening in the ground, pulling the coach down with them.

The two horses and the coach crashed onto the rocky floor at the bottom of the deep crevasse. The Prince was tossed about inside the coach as it broke free from the horses and bounced on the bottom. It toppled over several times before landing on top of Blaze and Glory, who were laying still. They had fallen hard, and were severely injured ... or worse.

Lord Ganador was a little bruised, but he was OK. He pulled himself out of the coach, eager to check on James and the horses.

Lord Ganador made a quick assessment of the situation, and knew James and Blaze and Glory were in serious trouble. The heavy coach was stuck on top of the two horses. As Lord Ganador looked up, he caught a glimpse of two ugly, troll-like creatures, peering down at him. They were standing close to the edge of the hole, snickering. As they giggled, they high-fived each other. They had gleefully watched as the horses, coach and Prince tumbled into the crevasse and crashed. Lord Ganador would deal with them later. Right now, he had more important things to take care of.

Lord Ganador knew James had fallen off the coach before it went tumbling down into the deep hole, and he couldn't see him. Blaze and Glory didn't look good at all. The Prince's Gold Crown had been knocked off his head when the coach hit bottom. It was tossed out of the coach, and had rolled behind a bunch of rocks. Also, his right, white glove had come off when he tried to grab the coach door to hang on.

Purity is Summoned

Lord Ganador wasn't concerned at all about his crown or his glove. He did care about James and the twin horses. He had to get the heavy coach off the horses right away. He blew his whistle loudly to summon Purity, who was already on his way to meet the Prince. He was being led by Peter and his two aides. They were almost to the base of the Mountain of Mist.

As soon as Purity heard his master's whistle, he knew that Lord Ganador was in trouble, so he pulled away from Peter and the aides. His wings lifted him straight up, and he flew over the forest to the other side. He spotted the gaping hole and deep ravine. He saw his Prince standing beside the crumbled coach, waving his arms. Purity stopped, mid-air, in disbelief, then quickly flew downwards and landed in front of his master. He dropped his head so Lord Ganador could grab his mane and the reins. The Prince pulled himself onto Purity's back, and they took off toward the top of the sink-hole to find James.

They flew along the edge of the hole, and found James lying on the meadow's grassy floor, right where the coach and horses went crashing into the deep crevasse.

James had passed out, but he was awake now, and two men from the village were attending to him. He was OK, and nothing appeared broken. They would take him to the village doctor to have him checked out. Lord Ganador already *knew* that James was OK.

Purity looked down over the edge of the gaping hole, and he saw his two beautiful sons pinned under the coach at the bottom. They were laying still, and he sensed they were dead. Purity threw up his head, reared, and let out a loud blowing snort. The Prince held on tight, and spoke softly to him, as he rubbed the side of the horse's neck. Purity shook his head, lifted his wings and flew back down to the coach. Ganador tossed the reins down, and jumped off Purity's back. He picked up the reins, and attached them securely, to the heavy coach. He signaled for Purity to back up, but as strong as this horse is, it was nearly impossible to lift the heavy, mangled coach off Blaze and Glory.

A Power Beam

Lord Ganador raised his right hand, and aimed it directly at Purity's wings. As he looked up to the sky, a glowing beam of red light, shot out from the palm of his un-gloved, right hand. The beam of light, shot

The Crash

lightning bolts of power through each wing and immediately, Purity lifted off the ground, pulling the heavy coach off his sons, Blaze and Glory. The Prince untied the reins from the coach, and he led Purity over to check on Blaze and Glory. They were still, and they were not breathing. Their necks were all twisted and broken. They had died instantly when they hit the rocky bottom.

Horse Tears

Purity nuzzled each of his sons, then shook his head, and cried out a mournful whinny. He backed away from Blaze and Glory. Lord Ganador rubbed Purity's neck and forehead and spoke calming words to try and comfort his horse. Then Lord Ganador left him, and walked over to Blaze and Glory. Before he bent down to check their pulses, he glanced back over his shoulder. He watched with compassion, as two big horse tears fell to the ground from Purity's soft and large, black eyes.

Healing Powers

As Lord Ganador's heart ached for his magnificent horse, he promised Purity that he would do, whatever he could, for Blaze and Glory. Purity looked deep into his master's kind eyes, and then dropped his head, and turned away. Lord Ganador turned back around, and knelt down beside the twin horses. He spoke soft, healing words over each horse, as he stroked their twisted necks, one at a time. He stood up and raised his right hand toward the grey, evening sky. Next, Lord Ganador waved his right arm over the two horses, and a glowing beam of red light came straight out from the middle of his palm. He waved this healing beam slowly, back and forth, over their broken bodies, while speaking soft words. Then, he concentrated on their broken necks. The warm, glowing beam of healing red light, was working. Lord Ganador kept speaking. His tone of voice was gentle but firm and commanding. Soon, Blaze and Glory started to breathe, very slowly, taking in deep breaths of air. As the healing beam continued moving back and forth, along their necks, it appeared to be massaging the muscles. The broken, twisted bones, visibly straightened, as the necks miraculously healed, and returned to normal.

Suddenly, Blaze and Glory stood straight up and shook themselves off, as if nothing had happened. They looked like they were waking up from a deep sleep. Purity pranced over to his sons and nuzzled them, sniffing and softly snorting, in gentle horse whispers. Purity turned to his master, Lord Ganador, and bowed before him, as if to say, "Thank-You." Next, he put his head against his master's chest, and gently nuzzled him. Lord Ganador responded by softly stroking Purity's head and ears. He grabbed his mane and the reins, and mounted him. Time to go for help. They would be back with fresh water and some strong men to help get Blaze and Glory and the mangled coach out of the deep ravine.

They flew up and stopped, where James was being helped onto one of the wagons. Once checked out by the Doctor, he would be taken back to the Bartletts' home.

Later, James checked out OK, and he was home, and resting.

The Rescue

Several of the strongest men had come to the crash site with heavy chains and ropes. They brought extra wagons and a heavy-duty tractor. Stable hands, from the Bartletts' barn, had brought special equipment and horse gear to help with the horses. The Prince was grateful for their help. Two buckets of water, from the Living Waters Stream, were handed to Lord Ganador, to take to Blaze and Glory. Purity and Ganador each took a quick drink of the cool water. It refreshed them. This crystal clear, cool water is pure, and has restorative powers.

The Prince grabbed the two buckets, and he and Purity flew them down to Blaze and Glory. As the horses drink their fill, the cool, refreshing water quickly energizes them.

Lord Ganador grabs the heavy ropes and chains, which had been thrown down to him. He worked hard to make sure that each rope and chain was safely secured to the coach. After he was certain they would hold, he took the loose ends of the ropes and chains, and attached them

The Crash

to the rope which he had tied around Purity's neck. He and Purity flew the ropes and chains up to the strong men. Lord Ganador kept two of the ropes tied around Purity's neck. The men each grabbed an end of rope or chain and held them tightly.

Ganador commanded Purity to raise up slowly. As soon as the slack was out of the ropes and chains, the strong men pulled as hard as they could, while Purity flew straight up. The coach was pulled upright. With the men's help, Purity carefully lifted the coach all the way up to the top, while the strong men pulled and set it down on the grassy area of the meadow.

It was a success. The heavy coach was battered, but intact. It was a very well-built coach. This task had taken close to an hour, and the strong men were pretty wiped out, so they each drank a glass of water from the stream and rested, but only for a couple of minutes.

It was time to go back down, and pull out Blaze and Glory.

Two heavy-duty, canvas horse hammocks (slings), harnesses and ropes, were lowered into the ravine. Purity and Lord Ganador flew back down to Blaze and Glory. Three stable hands lowered themselves down by heavy chains, which were hooked to the tractor. Once on the bottom, they all worked hard to secure the hammock slings around the middles of each horse. The harness straps were hooked to each sling.

Ropes were tied to the horses' halters, and their heads were then pulled to one side and secured to each hammock. This would prevent the horses from moving their heads. It looked bad, but it did not hurt them. It was for their safety and would protect their necks if they started to thrash their heads. Blinders were put over their eyes to prevent them from seeing. Horses don't always need to see where they're going.

The ropes and harness straps were tied around Purity's strong neck. The stable hands hooked the tractor chains to each horse hammock. When Lord Ganador gave his signal, Purity flew straight up, lifting the horses off the ground. The heavy-duty tractor backed up slowly, to make sure the horses were not injured, especially their necks. It was a miraculous feat, and one that would not be forgotten. Not anytime soon.

Finally, Blaze and Glory were safely at the top. They were freed from all the ropes, chains, harness straps, and hammock slings. The horse hammocks had securely held each horse, while they were being pulled straight up in the air, and flown to safety. Once on solid ground, the two stable hands hooked lead lines to each halter and removed the blinders. They walked the horses to calm them down. Soon, Blaze and Glory were happily grazing on the cool green grasses of Marion's Meadow.

Purity flew back down to get Lord Ganador and the three stable hands. The Prince mounted his horse, and the stable hands grabbed the three ropes, which were still tied around Purity's neck. They were lifted off the ground, and flown straight up to the top. What a thrilling flight that was for the stable hands!

Hats Off to the Prince

When everyone was safely back on top, the men all shouted, and threw their hats into the air, in celebration. When Ganador reached for his gold crown to toss it in the air, he remembered it was lost. With all the excitement, he had forgotten all about it and his missing white glove. Until that moment, no one else had noticed. Now they noticed. Instead of a gold crown, they saw the Prince's headband with red jewels encircling it. Interesting. Everyone wondered if that was what the Prince wore instead of the fancy crown whenever he wanted to dress more casual.

Some of the men were really curious now, and they watched as the red jewels, turned into blinking red lights. The Prince saw them staring at his headband, and he quickly mounted Purity. They flew back down into the ravine to search for his white glove and gold crown. As they were heading downward into the hole, a misty grey cloud came out of the woods and slithered down the bank of the deep ravine to meet them. The men at the top, watched in shock. They shouted to the Prince, to warn him. Suddenly, two icky-black Skanksters slid down the bank and into the ravine, and disappeared behind a rock.

As Purity and Lord Ganador were searching along the rocky bottom, the two Skanksters jumped out from behind the rock, where they had

The Crash

hidden. One of them had a white glove. He waved it in front of Purity, who immediately reared. The Prince almost fell off. He settled his horse, and watched the two Skanksters trying to scurry back up the bank. They were tripping over Ganador's white glove, and they kept tumbling back down.

Lord Ganador raised his right hand, and shot a beam of red light at them. They froze and stiffened into gnarly black shapes. They could not move. Ganador jumped off Purity and walked over to the two icky black creatures. He bent down, picked up his white glove, and shook the dirt off. He put the glove back on his right hand and shot a bolt of red lightening from one of the jewels in his headband. It struck the Skanksters and they disintegrated. The men at the top had been watching. They clapped their hands and cheered.

Lord Ganador then spoke to the grey cloud, he commanded it to leave. As soon as he said, "Be gone, cloud," *POOF!* The misty grey cloud vanished. He continued walking along the bottom, searching for his gold crown.

Blaze and Glory were being led back to the Bartletts' barn. It was a long walk, but it would be good for them, especially after what they'd been through. It would help clear their minds. Purity flew up quickly, to bid his sons farewell. The twin horses stopped. The three horses nuzzled, and whinnied their goodbyes. Blaze and Glory turned, and were led away.

Time to Bid Farewell

Purity flew back down to help his master search for the royal crown. After some time, they find it. It was behind the rocks, where it had rolled when the coach crashed. Lord Ganador dusts off his crown and places it on his head, over the blinking red-lights. He mounts Purity, and together, they fly back up to say goodbye to all the good men who had shown up to help.

The men are gathering their gear, and packing it into the remaining wagon. The Prince is grateful to them, and he thanks them for their courage and willingness to help. The men offer to help search for the Bright-Lights. They promise to contact the prince whenever—and if ever—they find any.

As the men bow to Lord Ganador, he sternly warns them, "Stay away from Skanky Pond, and keep your eyes out for the Skanksters. They are evil beings, capable of seriously hurting anyone they choose, including your children, your pets, and your property. They will destroy this good valley, the Dale of Derby, if they get the chance. That is their master's plan."

Then, Lord Ganador promises to return again someday. It is really late now, and dark. He must go. They understand, and shout, "Farewell, good Prince." He tips his royal crown and gives them another peek at his blinking red lights.

Purity and Lord Ganador plan to have a short rest on top of the Mountain of Mist, and Shimmer Lake. The Prince will leave, before the first light of day, to make it back to Evermore, on time for his next important assignment.

Purity lifts off the ground, with his powerful wings. Lightning flashes carry the horse and his Prince, straight up into the dark night's sky. The folks watch in amazement. All of a sudden, Purity turns right back around, and hovers over the crevasse. He passes over the giant hole, back and forth, three times. Lightning bolts and red light beams flash over the huge opening. On the third pass, the ground rumbles and the hole closes. The ground looks just as it did before, with no trace of the sink-hole.

Lord Ganador and his horse are finished here. At least for now. They flash-forward to the Mountain of Mist. Soon, lightning bolts, red glowing beams, and blinking red lights display their glory and light up the mountainside. As soon as they reach the top, the show ends and the lights go out, disappearing into the nighttime sky.

The Crash

Back at Darcy's garden, the last of the guests had left. Aunt Jenny, Ruthie, and Darcy had cleared the tea tables and put everything in the kitchen to be washed and put away. It was late.

Holy-Hocks and Hydrangel rounded up their woodland friends, and prepared to make their way home to the Stickety Wicket Woods. It was already quite dark, and nighttime is never a good time to travel. Darcy tries to talk them into spending the night in the garden, where they would be safe. The critters agreed to stay over. However, it has been a long, exciting day, and the two fairies just wanted to get home to their snuggly fairy houses and sleep in their own comfy beds. Darcy understands, but she is concerned and warns them to be very careful. It's just not safe to be out at night, especially when there could be a no-good menacer out and about. She reminds the fairies to protect their wings necklaces. Darcy lifts them up, and gives each of them a tender hug. Holy-Hocks and Hydrangel plant soft, fairy-tickle kisses on Darcy's cheek. Then Darcy gets a brilliant idea. She will send Annabelle and Clover with Holy-Hocks and Hydrangel. They can ride on top of Annabelle. This way, they will get back to the woods much more quickly and safely. Clover, being a good scout, will keep her sharp eyes out for any menacers. Excited, Annabelle wags her tail, does a couple of quick puppy circles, and jumps up and down. Clover gives everyone her snooty cat look, and they head out into the dark night toward the woods.

The royal tea party had been a huge success. Darcy and the fairies had received their beautiful angel wings necklaces and all had ended well. Except, of course, for the surprise sinkhole, the coach crash, the bruised driver, James, and the two dead horses, Blaze and Glory.

"All's Well That Ends Well"

* The party had ended well, and no one, other than Blaze and Glory, was seriously hurt in the crash, and even that tragedy had ended well.

Tales from Darcy's Garden

* Blaze and Glory were healed by Lord Ganador's healing beam of red light and are back in their stables, all cleaned up, well fed, and asleep.
* James Bartlett was OK'd by the village doc, and he is home resting.
* Blinking red lights had done away with two of the Skanksters.
* Lord Ganador had found his right, white glove and his royal crown. He and Purity are on their way home to Evermore.
* The Gala Coach is back at the Bartletts' barn and will be repaired.
* Darcy, Ruthie, and Aunt Jenny are in their pajamas, ready for bed. They will wait up for Annabelle and Clover to get back home from taking Holy-Hocks and Hydrangel back to their homes in the Stickety Wicket Woods. It shouldn't be too long of a wait.
*All the critters are safe in their garden hideouts, sleeping. Twinx and Taloop are sound asleep in the rose bushes, dreaming about Holy-Hocks and Hydrangel.

So, "All's Well that Ends Well."

Still Waiting for Annabelle and Clover to Return Home

Chapter 7

Moonlight Stroll

Annabelle and Clover left Darcy's garden with Holy-Hocks and Hydrangel and they had made it halfway across Marion's Meadow without any trouble. But as they get close to the duck pond in Devonshire Park, Holy-Hocks decides she wants to see if any of the ducks are still swimming in the pond. Clover has a hissy-fit. Holy-Hocks flicks off Annabelle's back and heads directly toward the pond. Hydrangel knows this isn't a good idea and demands that Holy-Hocks get back on top of Annabelle. Holy-Hocks has either just turned deaf or she's pretending to be. Clover wonders how she is supposed to protect the fairies when Holy-Hocks is completely out of control and temporarily out of her mind as well. Doesn't everybody know that ducks don't swim in the dark?

Annabelle starts to whimper and Hydrangel is losing her balance and starts crying. The cat threatens to leave them if they don't straighten up. Then all of a sudden, Clover spots something dark and icky heading towards the duck pond and Holy-Hocks. The cat stands straight up on both her hind legs and lets out a warning yowl. Annabelle jumps while Hydrangel sobs and holds on for dear life. Clover slumps down into the tall meadow grass and starts stalking the icky thing. There's nothing like an angry cat on the prowl. Cats are stealthy and superior hunters who can out-prowl most dogs.

CLOVER STALKS A SKANKSTER

Just as the icky Skankster is about to grab Holy-Hocks, Clover pounces and hits her target. The black menacer is snatched up and caught between Clover's teeth. Hydrangel proudly exclaims, "Great catch Clover. Way to go." Clover clamps her teeth deeper into the nasty Skankster, and shakes it hard, whacking it on a rock over and over again. This is doing serious bodily harm to the icky thing. Jeepers, it tastes absolutely disgusting! Clover is tempted to drop it. She wants to chew on some fresh clover *right now,* to rid her mouth of the putrid taste. This kitty knows she must finish the dirty job, so no matter how disgusting the Skankster tastes, her loyalty to her friends matters more. She finishes the job, walks over to the duck pond, and purposely tosses the lifeless ickiness into the water. Several little fish jump out of the pond and Clover gets her reward.

Before she takes the first bite of the fish, she has to clean her mouth. Annabelle and the fairies praise Clover, but she ignores them. She's chewing the meadow clover to freshen her mouth. Yucks! She wishes

Moonlight Stroll

she never has to taste another Skankster ever again. Now, she's ready to eat her yummy, fishy reward.

Holy-Hocks flickers over to Annabelle and settles down on her back and gives Hydrangel a hug. She realizes she'd made a big mistake which could have led to a tragic end. With tears in her eyes, Holy-Hocks vows to never try anything that stupid again. She apologizes to Clover and thanks her profusely. Clover purrs sweetly in response. She's a happy cat right now with a full fishy belly and fresh fishy breath. Mmmm!

It's time to get moving, and the little troop marches boldly towards the Stickety Wicket Woods entrance. They are so close and if there are no more encounters, they will be in the woods in a matter of minutes.

The full moon is peeking its bright face over the forest tree tops, while stars twinkle in the dark night's sky. The moonlight and starlight make it easier to see in the dark. Cats and dogs see pretty well in the dark, and Darcy had counted on Clover and Annabelle to get the fairies home safely and to protect them from any bad things. Since Clover had visited the fairies many times, she knows exactly where they live. Annabelle had never visited the fairies in the forest, so she depends on the cat to watch where they're going. The pup keeps her nose to the ground picking up *fairy-feet* scents. Suddenly, Annabelle's nose is distracted by a sudden stink followed by a scary noise.

A growling howl sounds from deep within the middle of the forest. Holy-Hocks and Hydrangel know they need to keep moving at a much faster pace than they are right now. A smelly grey cloud is slithering its way out of the swamp and into the forest. Holly-Hocks declares, "That was a *full* moon we just saw out in the meadow, peeking over the tree tops." They agree and they all know what it means. The fairies start to fear-shiver. *Fairy fear-shivers* feel just like flea bites to Annabelle, and she stops to scratch. Clover tells them to keep moving. As soon as the fairies stop shivering, Annabelle stops scratching and they enter the forest. It is much darker inside the woods, but Clover is well equipped with sight and Annabelle's nose keeps tracking the scent.

Tales from Darcy's Garden

Suddenly Clover screams an ear-piercing, warning yowl. She had just seen an icky black thing dash behind a tree. She encourages Annabelle to move forward and to pick up the pace. Immediately, Annabelle lowers her nose to the ground and quickly picks up the scent of fairy feet. They must move fast and stay on this path if they want to get the fairies home safe and sound.

Earlier today, Holly-Hocks and Hydrangel had travelled this same path, as they headed to Darcy's garden for tea time. They hadn't been able to flicker-fly because of the morning's dew, which had made their wings too wet and heavy. Thankfully, their tiny fairy feet had left enough of a scent for Annabelle to track. With her nose to the ground, Annabelle confidently takes the lead, while Clover stays alert, scanning their surroundings for any more menacers from the Skankster Gang.

While continuing on the path, a white squirrel jumps off a tree branch and lands right in front of Annabelle. She stumbles sideways and Holy-Hocks and Hydrangel fall off her back and land with a thud. Clover helps the fairies back up on Annabelle. Fuzz, the white squirrel, is friendly and he didn't mean to scare them. The fairies have known him a long time. He's a forest policeman who patrols the woods for lawlessness.

Clover had a run in with the Fuzz awhile back. While patrolling the forest, the Fuzz caught Clover robbing a critter. A woodland bird had caught a small fish from the duck pond, and carried it off to the forest in the hopes of eating it in peace. Clover just happened to be walking near the bird during a hunger spike. She couldn't control the urge and she snatched the fish away from the bird. The forest has laws against stealing food from woodland critters, so Fuzz gave Clover a very stern warning and a ticket.

News always travels fast inside the forest and Fuzz tells them he had heard the chatter about Clover getting rid of a Skankster, earlier. He tells the cat, "You have made Marskank extremely angry and he wants revenge. You need my help getting Holy-Hocks and Hydrangel home safely, so I will escort you." Clover shrugs and says, "Whatever."

Moonlight Stroll

Officer Fuzz joins them and they continue on the path to Holy-Hocks and Hydrangel's houses. Several woodland critters join them as well. Since there is safety in numbers, the critter company and the Fuzz Patrol escort is greatly appreciated. The stink-cloud and the howl disappears, and the rest of the walk home turns out to be a pleasant Moonlight stroll in the woods with friends.

Holy-Hocks and Hydrangel are home at last. They flicker off Annabelle's back and give her and Clover several fairy-hugs. They thank the Fuzz and all the critters for the escort. They are grateful to be home, safe and sound.

Years ago, when Holy-Hocks and Hydrangel arrived at the Stickety Wicket Woods forest, it seemed like an enchanting place to live for a while. It was nothing like the glorious and peaceful home they had just left, but they had a lot of hope and they hoped this forest would make them a peaceful and safe place to live, temporarily. They hadn't intended to live here for very long, but a dark and evil presence had kept them from returning to their real home far, far away from here. Bright memories of their home sweet home had slowly turned into fading dreams of "Another Place at Another Time." They began to feel homesick.

Shortly after they had arrived at these woods, the fairies met curious and friendly woodland critters who offered to help them build their shelters. The simple shelters soon turned into beautiful and charming fairy houses made from all the goodness that the forest provided at that time.

Holy-Hocks and Hydrangel wanted their fairy houses built right next to each other, with a little pathway in between, so they could visit each other and not have to go very far to do so. Holy-Hocks and Hydrangel have always been very close, just like sisters. After talking with many of the woodland critters back then, they were introduced to Fuzz.

Fuzz is not only a forest policeman, but also a certified forest house designer. He builds and renovates woodland and fairy houses in his spare time. Holy-Hocks and Hydrangel contracted with Fuzz, and right away, he started designing their spectacular fairy houses.

49

Once the plans had been approved by Holy-Hocks and Hydrangel, he and several critters began to construct them. Each house was uniquely different and designed specifically for each fairy. Their houses are tucked into the soft green mosses and roots of a huge Hemlock tree. He never builds two houses alike. Fuzz had crafted each fairy house with leaves, moss, twigs, mushrooms, acorn caps, and other woodsy stuff.

Every house that Fuzz had built was masterfully disguised and blended into the forest landscape. They were totally invisible to anyone—except, of course, Fuzz and his trusted woodland helpers. Woodland creatures know it's not good to live in the open where they might be seen. One never knows when something evil might be lurking in the forest. Every woodland creature, including the fairies, needs a safe zone to hide themselves, and all forest homes built by the Fuzz are certified safety zones.

The fairies are so happy to be home. The Fuzz and Clover check to make sure everything is OK. As soon as they are confident that Holy-Hocks and Hydrangel are home safe, Fuzz gives the "all clear."

Time for Annabelle and Clover to head back home. Darcy, Ruthie, and Aunt Jenny must be worried sick by now. The cat and pup had been gone far too long. Clover was anxious to get back to the comfort of Aunt Jenny's lap, and Annabelle looked forward to sleeping at the foot of Darcy's bed.

"Let's go," yowled Clover, impatient with Annabelle's long good-byes to everyone. Sometimes that dog could really get under Clover's fur. This cat has no patience with proper manners, or politeness. She's a cat, and that's that. Clover thinks very highly of her own "self-ness." She doesn't need anybody to "make *her* day." Nor does she care what anyone else thinks about her. She's very proud of who she is and her feline independence.

There are very few times when Clover can't catch her own food, but when she can't and she gets really hungry, she will lower her standards and be nice to the human subjects who serve her. She will purr

Moonlight Stroll

and rub against her subject's leg, but only until the cat food bowl is laid at her feet.

Sometimes she'll rub up against Annabelle, but never as a friendly gesture.

She does this to distract the dog, and steal some of the pup's tasty food. Annabelle never seems to mind. She loves Clover, and is happy to share her food with her feline friend. Not so, the other way around. No! If Annabelle even tries to grab a piece of Clover's food, a cat's-claw comes out of her cat's-paw, and scratches the pup's wet nose with a quick cat-smack.

This finicky feline isn't what you would call warm, sweet, or cuddly. But, she is a fierce warrior, and will protect her friends with her life, if need be. Clover must have had heard about cats having nine lives; she takes a lot of risks. She's an excellent huntress. Many nights she'll venture out on a prowl to catch and kill rogue rodents, poisonous snakes, lizards, and other creepy critters. She never eats them though. Instead, she'll carry them to her humans in exchange for canned tuna.

The one thing she hates the most is catching and killing the Skanksters. They taste so horrible she sometimes *yuck-chucks*. Clover catches them anyway, and is proud of herself for doing so. This cat isn't totally selfish, she's just an independent opportunist. Clover, along with some of her friends and the buzzards, do a great job keeping the icky Skanksters out of the village.

Right now, Clover has grown impatient, still waiting on Annabelle to finish saying her long "goodbyes" to the fairies, and each and every other critter as well. You would think there was nothing better for the pup to do. Clover meowed one "Goodbye," and that was that. She saunters off toward the path leading back to the forest entrance. One thing about cats, they have no patience, and Clover's patience had run out. She is heading home, *right now*. Annabelle will just have to catch up.

Hopefully, she won't get lost.

Annabelle finally finishes her goodbyes and she is ready to head back home. She turns toward Clover, but the cat is not there. She had already left, and was out of sight. With Annabelle's keen sense of smell, she should be able to find the right path. She is certain she'll catch up with the cat.

As soon as Annabelle steps onto the path however, the scent smells funky. Apparently too many footprints from all the other critters, who had joined them earlier, made for a miss-mash of smells. Now Annabelle isn't sure which way to turn. This worries the pup, and she begins to turn in circles, trying desperately to pick up Clover's or even the *fairy-feet* scent.

Finally, she thinks she has the cat's scent and she turns right. She follows this path, until it comes to a crossing, and the scent completely disappears. She doesn't know which way to turn and nothing looks familiar. On the way into the forest, it was Clover whose eyes watched where they were going, while Annabelle just kept her nose to the ground.

Not knowing which way to turn, Annabelle steps off the path to rest. She finds a soft patch of moss to lie down on and she quickly falls into a deep sleep. Moments later, an icky-black creature stumbles upon the sleeping pup and lets out a hideous howl. It jumps on top of Annabelle's head and bites her in the face. Annabelle wakes up abruptly and she lets out a loud, painful yelp. She sees a dark, icky creature staring her in the face. She jumps up, bares her teeth and growls, as fierce as she can. She tries to catch the ugly menacer, but it is too quick for her. It chomps down on Annabelle's back leg, seriously injuring her. All of a sudden a mighty wind, rushes through the forest trees, and what looks like a small Indian-being with wings, appears. He shoots an arrow straight through the Skankster's chest, pinning it to the ground. It lays there squirming and writhing in pain, while oozing its black ickiness onto the green, mossy ground.

Annabelle slowly pulls herself up and tries to run away. She can't stand and she falls back down. She is in terrible pain and cannot move. She starts to whimper.

Chapter 8

Winged Blue Beings

A winged, blue being walks toward Annabelle. She can see him, but not very well. She's frightened and cannot move. Then, a beautiful blue female being with wings appears. She looks similar to the fairies, only bigger. The Indian-being who had arrow-shot the Skankster calls the female being, Princess Mortania. She tells her Indian companion to bring her some poison ivy vines for the dog's wounds. Mortania calls her companion, Chief Two-Feathers.

Terrified, Annabelle trembles; she whimpers. She can hear and smell the blue beings, but she can barely see them. She lets out a really loud and frightened bark. Her back leg, her face and eyes are starting to swell, badly. The Skankster's venom is poisoning this precious pup. She's going blind, and her rear leg is swollen, bleeding, and motionless. She's in unbearable pain.

In a matter of minutes, Two-Feathers reappears with the ivy vines. Mortania gently covers the pup's face and rear leg with the medicinal leaves. Normally, this plant is poisonous and causes swelling and red, itchy blisters on most humans, but on critters and forest folks, it has a healing effect. It begins drawing the venomous poison out of Annabelle's body. Soon, the swelling starts going down, but she still can't stand up, and everything looks grey and cloudy.

Annabelle is still in terrible pain and is helpless. She is at the mercy of these two beings. Chief Two-Feathers bends over the pup. He takes his broken half-feather out of the pouch that hangs on his neck. He waves this half-feather over Annabelle's body, while chanting words she doesn't understand. As he softly chants, Annabelle feels the pain leaving her weary body. She stops whimpering and her body quits trembling.

She is no longer frightened. She senses that these two blue beings are helping her. She licks Two-Feathers' hand. He gently pets her and says, "Good pup, you're OK." Annabelle understands these words.

Princess Mortania pulls a beautiful, golden trumpet out of her back-pack. She puts the trumpet to her mouth and sounds off a loud warning. This trumpet warning will summon her tribe, the Moratores, and all of the other Bright-Light tribes living in the woods and elsewhere in the Dale.

Holy-Hocks and Hydrangel are still standing outside their houses, talking, when they hear the trumpet's warning. Instinctively, they touched their wings necklaces and head toward the trumpet's blaring sound. There is danger in the forest. They must go and offer their help.

Holy-Hocks and Hydrangel call for Clover, but get no response; she is already too far away to hear them. Next, they called Annabelle's name. She responds with a whimper and a loud bark. They know she's in trouble. They quickly flicker off in the direction of the trumpet's blare, and as soon as they arrive, they were astonished to see two blue-skinned, Elfin-like winged beings caring for their beloved Annabelle.

Princess Mortania and her trusted sidekick, Chief Two-Feathers, are leaders of a small tribe of Bright-Lights. They are winged, blue beings called the Moratores. Two-Feathers is a bit of a renegade, but he has always been an excellent scout and he is still a mighty warrior, just like his beloved princess. He is called Two-Feathers because that's all the feathers he has left on his headdress. He used to have a full-feathered headdress, like many of the other chiefs in his tribe who came before

Winged Blue Beings

him. However, too many wars had taken place over the ages, and most of his feathers had been destroyed, or taken in battle.

When all of the other chiefs in the Moratore Tribe had passed on, Princess Mortania appointed Two-Feathers to Chiefdom. Two-Feathers is getting a little older and slower now, but Mortania always trusts his wisdom, his loyalty, his strength and his unwavering courage. Chief Two-Feathers had always been a great warrior, but because of his *Unruly Tempers,* he had lost all but two and a half of his feathers in many battles that were of his own choosing. The two remaining feathers on the chief's headdress are still strikingly beautiful.

The feather in front of his headdress stands straight up, alert at all times. Chief calls this feather "Scout." The second feather on back of his headdress, hangs straight down. Chief calls this feather "Number Two." No one knows about the half feather except Princess Mortania. Chief keeps the half feather in a leather pouch, which hangs on his very thick neck. Chief Two-Feathers often uses this feather to perform various charms and healing spells. He calls it "Half-Feather."

Number Two hangs straight down, and will point in whichever direction "Scout" feather urges it to.

Whenever Chief Two-Feathers or anyone else in his tribe are facing danger, straight up "Scout" will glow, and Number Two will quiver and then point in the direction "Scout" urges it to. Scout's direction always leads to safety.

This early warning detection system is a powerful gift from Evermore. This has been protecting the Chief and his Princess, and all the other Bright-Lights through the ages.

On the day Princess Mortania appointed Two-Feathers to Chiefdom, she held a special ceremony. She had summoned the tribes with her trumpet. She lifted her three-stringed Bow and called down the Powers of Evermore. A flashing bolt of lightning came straight down through the tree-tops and struck Two-Feathers' headdress. Immediately, his two feathers lit up and a powerful glow filled the Stickety Wicket Woods. Both Scout and Number Two quivered and then became still.

It was an awesome ceremony. Chief never takes this gift for granted. He has become a mighty, but humble and grateful, warrior.

Whenever the Scout and Number Two feathers are on high alert, the Chief will lead his Princess and the Bright-Light Tribes to safety, following in the direction Number Two points to.

When Number Two feather points straight back down and is still, it means "All Is Well."

Chief Two-Feathers is the last standing chief of the great Moratore Tribe.

Chapter 9

The Bright-Light Tribes

Holy-Hocks and Hydrangel are now tending to their beloved Annabelle. The pup can't see and her leg is stiff, but all the pain is gone from her body. She tries to get up and it takes her a moment, but she is able to stand. Her cloudy eyes make it hard to see, but her nose lets her know where her two fairy friends are. She cuddles up to them and wags her tail, and lick-kisses them.

Hopefully, she'll get her sight back soon. At least she can walk and even with a limp, she's getting around pretty good. Her nose is working even better than before, and she is totally out of pain.

Holy-Hocks and Hydrangel thank Princess Mortania and Chief Two-Feathers for caring for Annabelle and for saving her life. They stay beside the pup, and will not leave her. Princess Mortania's trumpet is still summoning the tribes.

The Moratores

Moratores are the cherished leaders and fierce protectors of the Bright-Lights Tribe. They are led by Chief Two-Feathers and Princess Mortania. This is a small tribe of winged blue beings. Each Moratore has a circle of glowing light, surrounding their dragonfly-shaped wings. There are only twelve members, including the Chief and his Princess. Moratores are skilled, powerful, and very brave warriors.

The Moratores don't live in the woods, but they are still referred to as forest folks. They live just outside The Stickety Wicket Woods, in a place called Stones Throw, a hilly and rocky area at the base of the Mountain of Mist, near the northeast entrance to the woods.

The Moratores live in small tree houses, tucked into the huge chestnut trees. These ancient chestnut trees grow in the hilly and rocky area of Stones Throw. The Moratores live in the chestnut trees with their war birds, known as the Thunder Birds. These large, blue-black birds have fancy top-knots, adorned with brightly colored battle beads. Right now, the Moratores are flying into the forest, on their Thunder Birds, armed and ready for battle.

All Moratores, male and female wear armor of heavy, metal shields and helmets. They each carry their favorite weapons. Some carry spears, some carry bows and arrows, others carry hatchets and heavy stone mallets. Not one of them have feathers or weapons, like their chief or his princess.

The beautiful blue females have long sandy-blond or bright-red hair, which they wear in two braids. Each braid is woven with colorful battle beads. The blue males have long and shiny black hair, worn in one thick braid and also woven with battle beads.

Princess Mortania has long flowing red hair and she never wears a helmet. During battles, she wears her mother's battle-beaded braid as her headdress. Mortania had cut this braid from her mother's hair on the day she had passed. Mortania's dress and boots are made from deer-skin, and her necklace has been made with the colorful battle beads. She is carrying her powerful three-stringed bow and magic arrows, for this upcoming war.

Chief Two-feathers has long, black flowing hair. His battle beads are sewn onto his two-feathered headdress. His pants and vest are made out of grey-wolf skins. His high, fringed boots are made from black-wolf skins. He is carrying his mighty bow and a quiver full of magical arrows.

The Chief and his Princess, along with all the other Moratores, have colored their faces with war-paint. They are waiting for their Princess and her Chief to deliver the battle orders.

The Princess and her Chief are discussing the Rules of Engagement while waiting for the rest of the Bright-Lights to arrive for the meeting.

The Heart-Light Fairies

Traveling north, along the forest path are the Heart-Light fairies, just like Holy-Hocks and Hydrangel. There are males as well as females. These tiny, butterfly-winged beings are the only members of the Bright-Lights Tribe, who have the glowing Heart-Lights and are fiercely protected by the Moratores. The little Heart-Light fairies are ready for battle and their powers have been restored by the angel wings necklaces.

Many of the Heart-Light fairies are riding on top of their favorite forest critters. Some are on squirrels and chipmunks, while others are on fluffy bunnies and the soft grey mice. Some are flying on glitter birds. Their Heart-Lights are glowing bright again, filling the woods with golden, twinkling lights. It's a wonderful sight to see. Holy-Hocks and Hydrangel are so excited to see the other fairies and they flutter off to join them, with Annabelle hobbling close behind. The pup could actually see the glowing heart-light flickers and this makes the pup happy.

Annabelle catches the whiff of a cat and it smells fishy, just like her kitty friend. She can't see Clover, but she sure hopes and prays it is her. Annabelle wasn't sure if the cat had made it back to Darcy's garden, or if she had been caught, and hurt, just like she had been.

As a matter of fact, Clover had made it back to the garden safely. That had been a while ago. Almost as soon as the cat entered the garden gate, she heard the trumpet's warning blast and she knew immediately that there was trouble in the woods. It was a cry for help. She thought of Annabelle. Clover knew she had to get back. She ran over to the Rose bushes and got Twinx and Taloop out of their beds. Clover was the only one who had seen them there earlier. The two fairies hopped on top of the cat and off they fled, back to the Stickety Wicket Woods. A quick stop at the duck pond and a quick bite of fish, and Clover is ready to continue.

When Clover enters the forest with Twinx and Taloop, she's amazed at what she sees. One area is lit up like a huge Christmas tree. It's all of the Heart-Light Fairies and their sparkling heart-glows. At the first sound of the trumpet's warning, Holy-Hocks and Hydrangel had touched their wings necklaces and the Powers of Evermore returned to this tribe.

Clover marches up to the Heart-Lights and nods her head at them. With Twinx and Taloop still on her back, she gallantly leads this glowing tribe of Heart-Lights to the Battle Camp Meeting. As soon as she sees Holy-Hocks, Hydrangel and Annabelle, she stops and drops Twinx and Taloop off her back, and runs right over to the pup. She softly meows, purrs and rubs herself against Annabelle. Clover is so happy to see her best friend. When she notices that Annabelle had been wounded, it makes her angry, and she promises Annabelle she will never leave her like that ever again. She is truly sorry. In fact, she feels so badly a tear drops from one of her big green eyes and lands on top of Annabelle's paw. The

The Bright-light Tribes

pup licks the cat's tear off her paw and she sits back down. Annabelle is happy to have Clover back by her side.

Chapter 10

The Not So Bright-Lights Tribes

The Half-Lits

The Half-Lits are pudgy little gnome-like forest folks. They have round bellies, red cheeks, and jolly good natures. The males have long white curly hair and beards. The plump gals wear their hair anyway they want, and any color they choose. The Half-Lits are extremely humorous, and they are known as *jolly-good* folks. They are wingless beings.

These jolly-good folks love their simple life in a place called Happy Hollow, which is located in the Old Woods section in the Northwest corner of the Stickety Wicket Woods. The Old Woods section is where some of the dead trees from the Ancient Forest can still be found.

The jolly-good fellas love to drink a special juice, which they make from very rare mushrooms. This "shroom juice," as they call it, has a rather interesting effect on the Half-Lit fellas. They have to be very careful and control their cravings for this juice. A little of it goes a long way. A little too much of it and corny, senseless joking, and crazy dancing happens. The Half-Lits love corny jokes, crazy dancing, and having fun.

The Not So Bright-lights Tribes

A small band of Half-Lit jolly-good fellas, known as Mushers, travel deep into the forest, on what they call Mush-Hunts. The lead Mush-Hunter is Harry Q. Bindlestick (better known as Uncle Harry). He knows exactly where to find the special red and white, spotted mushrooms. They grow under the mossy damp ground, next to the huge forest Hemlock trees. The Mushers dig up these rare mushrooms, using small red, or green, handled shovels, also known as trowels. They carry these small shovels by looping them onto their belts with leather strings.

Mush-Hunters carry the dug-up mushrooms in woven grass sacks, which are tied around beautiful crooked sticks and carried over their shoulders.

Crooked Sticks

The crooked sticks which the Mushers and all the other jolly-good fellas use, have been made from dead tree branches, found in the ancient old woods section of the forest. The ancient dead trees were nearly petrified, which made the branches difficult to work with. Once the bark was scraped off, the crooked wooden sticks were beautiful. The Mushers and jolly-good fellas scraped all the bark off the sticks with their pocket knives. They always carry these knives in their back pockets. They had to sharpen the knives often with the roughest stones they could find.

Once the bark was completely removed, the fellas had carved beautiful art-work on the thickest end of the stick (the handle end). Each crooked stick was then rubbed to a golden finish, with a special dye made from Maple tree bark. These are beautiful crooked sticks and the jolly-good fellas are very proud of them, and all the creative artwork they had done on the handles. Each design is different and no two sticks are alike.

When these crooked sticks aren't being used to carry the mushroom-filled grass-sacks, they are used for other purposes. For example, if a Musher drinks too much shroom juice, these beautiful crooked sticks will help them to walk a straight line, and also help them to stay up-right.

63

After hours of digging, and they have gathered enough mushrooms to fill their grass-sacks, the Mushers carry the rare mushrooms back through the woods and drop them off at the Happy Hollow Pub.

Uncle Harry and his four brothers own the Happy Hollow Pub, a warm and cozy, tucked away, eatery and juice bar. The Happy Hollow Pub is inside an ancient, hollowed-out log. Harry's four brothers had found this great old log and they had decided to hollow it out and then they turned it into a delightful Pub. It's a happy place to eat, drink, and be merry and it even has a great dance floor.

Harry's wife, Geezle, is fully-rounded, and she's a jolly-good cook. She has a couple of gals to help her in the kitchen. Breakfast, lunch and supper are served Monday through Friday. The pub's Saturday Night Special is tasty: canned tomato soup with grilled cheese sandwiches.

Uncle Harry tends his Juice Bar on Friday and Saturday nights, while his brother's band, the Sha-room Four, sing and play happy dancing music. One of the brothers plays drums, one plays guitar, and one plays Harmonica or Fiddle, and the last of the brothers, sings and plays Banjo.

The Not So Bright-lights Tribes

The Happy Hollow Pub is the best place to go for jolly-good food, jolly-good music, and jolly-good dancing. On Friday and Saturday nights, the Happy Hollow Pub is a lively, *jump-jivin'* place. It is always closed on Sundays, so that all the jolly-good Half-Lits can attend the Little Brown Church in the woods. They always enjoy an up-lifting sermon, delivered by Bishop Bobble.

When a Half-Lit drinks a bit too much of the shroom juice, he becomes *fully lit*. This is when he'll need his Crooked stick to walk a straight line, should he get stopped by The Fuzz on his way home.

These pudgy, Half-Lit characters are plumper and shorter than any of the fairies, elves, or pixies. There are only twenty of these curious folks left, and twenty is plenty. Most of the good-fellas have wives or gal-friends. The older gals are a lot plumper than their jolly-good fellas, but that's just the way the jolly-good fellas like their gals. "The plumper, the better," the fellas always say.

The older jolly-good husbands and gents refer to their wives and older gals as Plumpettes. The older and wiser jolly-good wives and gals are very proud of their pudgy-ness, so being called a Plumpette is a term of endearment for them. The younger generation of gals, however, is not nearly as plump as the older jolly-good gals are, and they are not at all happy with the term Plumpette. They want to keep their girlish figures as long as they can and they prefer being able to fit into their cute and stylish Battle-Suits and look "hot" while on the battlefield. The younger Half-Lit dudes pretty much agree with them on this subject.

The two jolly-good leaders of the Half-Lits are, Boozle and his younger assistant, Dorf. Boozle used to carry a flask (a small bottle) filled with what he called "energy" juice in his back pocket. It was probably shroom juice, but no one ever asked him. Whenever Boozle thought he needed a boost of energy, he would pull out his flask and take a quick nip.

Boozle sure did get a lot of energy from his juice. His cheeks would turn a bright-red, and then he'd start to dance all by himself, with or without music. When he drank too much of his so-called "energy" juice, he would start *Crazy Dancing,* and this dancing was just too weird for anyone to have to watch. His wife Drizzle usually ignored Boozle when he got too *juiced or fully-lit.* She knew sooner or later he would pass out, and she would have to carry him home over her shoulders and put him to bed.

During one of the forest battles, Dorf had to take charge. Boozle had drunk too much of his "energy" juice and he had fallen asleep right in the middle of the battleground. He wasn't able to get up, so Dorf had to carry him off the battlefield. After that embarrassing incident, Boozle thought it best to appoint Dorf as his Second Lieutenant.

Dorf was much younger than Boozle and he could handle any battle on any battlefield. Dorf has himself a lovely, jolly-good and robust gal-friend named Squizzle. Together they enjoy their life in the forest and hope to be married one day.

Boozle's wife, Drizzle, loved her jolly-good husband very much. They were happily married, without children. When he'd had too much "energy" juice, she would tuck Boozle into their bed, kiss him good-night, and go out and fight his battles for him. She was an amazing warrior. While Boozle slept and dreamt, Drizzle fought. She fought and won many battles for him.

One evening, without her beloved Boozle beside her, Drizzle lost a battle. She had been hauled away and was never seen again.

After that, Boozle gave up all his battles and all his bottles. He also gave up his rank and made Dorf the Commander in Chief of the Half-Lit Tribe.

Boozle never came out of his house again ... until he heard the trumpet's call this night.

The Dim-Lits

The Muddlers belong to the Dim-Lits Tribe. Their hearts are not totally dark, but they have very little light left in them. It's hard to describe these wingless beings. Mostly, they look like icky trolls with warty bumps. They have little tufts of hair on top of their heads, on their

The Not So Bright-lights Tribes

butts, their noses, their toes and heels. They are dark grey, not black. They look like crackled and dirty mud-monsters.

Muddlers are Shape-Shifters and sometimes it is really hard to tell exactly what they do look like. They can shape themselves to look like a friendly forest critter, someone's pet dog or cat, or even a bird. They can only hold their alter-shape for about thirty minutes, which is long enough to trick somebody. They don't have the power to shape-shift into human beings, or any of the members of the Bright-Lights Tribes.

Muddlers have powers to cast illness spells, with special elixirs they make from poisonous plants. One time just for the fun of it, they had made a couple of village kids really sick. Although they can make somebody quite ill, they *cannot* seriously hurt them. They don't have the really bad powers; not yet anyway.

They're called Muddlers because they like to hang out in the Swamp, where they love to wrestle in the mud. Mud-wrestling is their work-out exercise. They are always preparing for battles, so they like to keep themselves fit. They love battles, even though they haven't won any—at least, not yet. They know a really big battle is coming. They don't know exactly when, but they want to be ready, fit and able, whenever the time does come.

Right up close to Skanky Pond, the ground is all wet and mucky. The Muddlers love to cover themselves with the rich black mud that is found there. After the mud dries, they look cracked and creepy, and yet they look quite harmless. They look like funny, ugly mud-monsters. Beware, for these creepy muddy creatures are very sneaky and they might fool you into thinking they won't hurt you. Remember, they can shape-shift into a friendly little critter, and trick you. They can also hurt you if ever, and whenever, they feel like it. If you see a Muddler, stay away from it.

The Muddler's leader, Gog-Mantle, and his Warrior Bride, Shivering Gritz, make a great mud-wrestling team. The two of them really enjoy rolling around in the mucky mud, practicing their mud-slinging skills. They like making mud-weapons of all sorts, but their favorite weapons to make are mud-pies. They like making mud-pies, because they make really great weapons once they dry. These mud weapons will put a hard-smacked hurt on somebody real quick. Gog-Mantle and Shivering Gritz have a full arsenal of mud-pies, mud-balls, and mud-wumps, which they store in several sunny areas of the forest. Once the mud-weapons are dry, they look like ordinary stones and rocks.

Mud-Wumps are swamp critters which Gog-Mantle and Shivering Gritz capture, and roll in the mud. Once the mud dries and hardens around the critter, they are ready to be used as weapons. It's not fun being a Mud-Wump. The name sounds cool, but that's about it. Once a Mud-Wump is thrown, and it hits the target, the hardened outer mud-shell cracks open and the poor creature inside is badly injured, or worse. Gog-Mantle and Shivering Gritz love using the Mud-Wumps for target practice. This fearless leader and his bride are far more ghoulish than most of the other Dim-Lits.

None of the Dim-Lits have any intentions of going to the Bright-Light's Battle Camp Meeting. In fact, when they heard the trumpet's blast, they retreated to the Swamp and the outer banks of Skanky Pond. They are busy revising their own battle plans and rules of engagement. They have put on their thickest mud armor, and they are ready for battle.

This will not be like any other forest battle. The Dim-Lits are prepared to show the Bright-Lights a thing or two. They have had it with these stuck-up goody-two-shoes. Who the heck do they think they are anyway? These Do-Gooders have been hiding in the woods for ages and they have been preying on the Dim-Lits with a vengeance.

Whenever a Muddler comes out of hiding just to do a bad thing, one of the Bright-Lights always tries to take them out, and they have many, many times. Truthfully, most of the Dim-Lit eliminations had been accomplished by that darn cat, Clover and her friends from the Cod-Swallop Dump, the Dump Dogs and Trash Cats.

Gog-Mantle and Shivering Gritz are going to do their very best, to get that cat, and any of her friends. Their main goal had always been, to put a serious hurt on Clover's stupid dog friend, Annabelle. Earlier, they

The Not So Bright-lights Tribes

had recruited one of the icky-black Skanksters to hurt the dog, and it did. But, then the menacer was killed by an arrow.

Also, earlier this evening, Gog-Mantle had gotten sweet revenge on the Royal Prince and the Bright-Lights. He'd known about the tea party in Darcy's garden. A Muddler disguised as a woodland critter had heard about the "secret party," and he had told Gog-Mantle about the event. So, Gog-Mantle and Shivering Gritz had made big plans to ruin the end of Darcy's big day. They watched for the Royal Gala Coach and as soon as it pulled up to Darcy's garden to pick up the Prince, Lord Ganador, they ran into Marion's Meadow and hid in the tall grasses.

Gog-Mantle and Shivering Gritz had patiently waited and watched. As soon as he saw his opportunity, Gog-Mantle alter-shaped into an icky-black thing and jumped right out in front of the twin horses and spooked them. They tripped and stumbled, and went tumbling into the new sink-hole. Somehow, the Darkled Dragon from Skanky Pond had just created that hole from way down deep beneath the earth's surface. Perfect timing.

When the two horses tripped and stumbled into the deep ravine that the sinkhole had created, the coach—along with Prince Ganador—landed on top of them. The horses had broken their necks and died. Gog-Mantle hadn't intended for Blaze and Glory to actually die. His main goal was to shake up the Royal Prince from Evermore, and watch him suffer. However, he did think the dead horses might be a big enough bonus to get him promoted. It certainly would make a good report to give Marskank. Perhaps Gog-Mantle would get his long overdue promotion. He was very proud of himself and he ran back into the woods laughing all the way. He couldn't wait to give the Dragon Lord the good news.

When the news hit the Swamp that Clover and Annabelle were bringing Holy-Hocks and Hydrangel back to the woods in the dark, it was Shivering Gritz's idea to recruit a Skankster to hurt Annabelle. She would do whatever she had to do to help Gog-Mantle get his promotion.

Shivering Gritz was sick and tired of being a Dim-Lit Muddler. She knew she was worthy of far greater battles than mud-slinging. Her deepest desire was to become a full-blown Skankster. Her long-time dream of becoming a Princess Warrior of the Darkled Tribe was going to come true, she would make sure of it.

When that trumpet blasted its warning, everything changed. Gog-Mantel and Shivering Gritz seized the opportunity and prepared for real *war*. They hoped to fight alongside the Skankster Gang, rather than with the Dim-Lit, mud-slinging Muddlers. They both have been superior warriors and deserved a much darker calling.

Chapter 11

The Darkled Dragon and His Black-Hearted Tribe

The Skanksters

The Darkled Dragon, Marskank, is the evilest tribal lord in existence. His icky, pond-scum, slime-bags, the Skankster Gang, are similar to the Dim-Lits, but they are far more evil and black-hearted. Their heart-lights had burnt out ages ago, long before they had come to the Stickety Wicket Woods. Their hearts had been eaten up with jealousy, hatred, envy, and pride. These folks are truly bad beings. Don't let their looks deceive you. They are true masters of the shape-shifting delusions. You must be very discerning (able to detect evil presence) and use the power of wisdom.

The Darkled Dragon has been confined to Skanky Pond for centuries, which has him in a foul mood every day of his dismal life. He is a very angry dragon, and he wants out of the pond. Now! He had tried to escape many times, but had failed. He always feels the need to hurt somebody. He thinks hurting somebody will make him feel better, but it never does. He's just plain hateful and angry all the time.

Anger and bitterness can make folks want to hurt others, and "misery loves company." Marskank is very angry and bitter, so he keeps company with those of the darker side. He definitely wants to hurt others and pull them into the darkness with him. He loathes all of the Bright-Lights, and anyone who has even the tiniest bit of goodness in them. He wants to destroy the light. His heart is black as night.

Fangle, a.k.a. Flat Fangle

Marskank trains his Skanksters to be dark and heartless, enabling them to do his evil biddings. The Bright-Light tribes had taken out many of his gang members and he is getting low on his supply. So, he continually sends Fangle into the forest to recruit members from the Dim-Lits tribe. He needs to replace his losses and increase his arsenal of vile menacers.

Most of the Dim-Lits aren't willing to join the Skanksters. They don't think they have the stomach to endure the gang's *Membership Initiation.* However, there's always a few who are "on the fence," and Fangle is able to convince them that the Dragon's rewards are worth jumping over to the darker side. With each new recruit, Fangle has risen in rank and he is now the leader of the Skankster Gang.

Fangle had been in an accident and instead of a black, troll-like Skankster creature, he now looks like a flat-headed, flat-bodied snake. He had gotten rolled over by the Bo-Peep's huge tractor tire. Fangle hadn't been paying attention. He'd gotten caught in one of the tire treads and he was dragged and rolled, over and over, through the Bo-Peep's pastures. His body never returned to its normal troll-like shape. Fangle now has tractor tire treads where his round, black warts used to be. Marskank had changed his name from Fangle to Flat Fangle. The Dragon Lord did this to make Fangle feel even worse than he already did. Marskank liked to keep Fangle feeling down and bad about himself.

Flat Fangle looks like a flat snake, but he doesn't slither on the ground like a snake does. He walks straight up on short stubby legs, with flat and hairy-toed feet. His arms have been mashed into his chest,

The Darkled Dragon And His Black-hearted Tribe

and only his hands are visible now, but they are totally useless. They just poke out of his chest and hang there, flapping in the breeze. His once round, fat head is now flat. His eyes are almost on top of each other, and his pointy nose is longer than before. His face looks really gross. His long fangs stick out his mouth, and his icky, yellow-spotted tongue won't roll back into it.

Flat Fangle is unglamorous, to say the least, and he has his own set of difficulties. It's really hard to eat when he can't pull his tongue back inside his mouth and his hands are useless. The "tractor tire transformation" had put Fangle into a deeper and darker funk. He is still fearless, though, and like most of the other icky menacers, he is always ready to do whatever the Darkled Lord commands. All of the Skanksters are willing to maim, curse, or *do away* with anyone, just to please Marskank. The Darkled Dragon seems to be winning more and more over to his black-hearted side.

Flat Fangle and the rest of the Skanksters Gang are looking forward to an all-out war, a real slime-bath. These hateful creatures have been preparing for ages to battle and win a war, leaving total devastation. The darkled ones hope to completely take over the Stickety Wicket Woods, the Mountain of Mist, and Shimmer Lake. They even hope to ruin the meadowlands and pollute the Living Waters Stream.

Marskank's deepest desire and long-term goal is to destroy the Royal Prince from Evermore. First, he will destroy Darcy's garden. The evil dragon and his Skanksters hate it, whenever others find peace and joy in Darcy's tea time and story-telling sanctuary. As a matter of fact, they hate the whole danged Dale of Derby, and everyone in it. They especially hate the Good Church and its Pastor. He's the one that is always warning the folks to be aware of the Evil One, the dark lord of "Under-earth."

It might take Marskank and his gang a while longer, but with enough recruits, he and the Skanksters are sure they will win the war, one battle at a time, if need be. They are confident that one day, they will rule the Dale, and beyond.

The Dragon and his Black-Hearted Tribe must win this war and destroy every one of the Bright-Lights before their Prince, Lord Ganador, returns with his mighty warriors from Evermore.

As soon as Mortania's trumpet blares, the Skanksters armor up, and ready themselves for what they hope will be a war of mass devastation.

These Darkled, otherworldly beings need to be gone. No one in this peaceful dale wants their kind of darkness.

How did they get here in the first place? They don't belong here, and they are *not* welcome!

But they are here, at least for now.

Chapter 12

A Bright-Light Battle-Camp Meeting

At the trumpet's first warning blast, the Bright-Light Tribes assemble and head to the Battle-Camp Meeting. The Moratores are already there. Next to come are the Heart-Light Fairies, with Holy-Hocks, and Hydrangel and Clover and Annabelle leading the way. Most of the woodland critters, and even a few of the Swampers are with them. The Bright Lights are in hopes that the Half-Lits Tribe will join them. They will wait a little bit because the Half-Lits are always late.

This small army of tiny folks doesn't look big enough to win a small argument, let alone a war against the Darkled Dragon and his gang. But these little warriors are a fearless bunch. None of the Dim-Lits are going to join the Bright-Lights, so they need the Half-Lits to come alongside them and help. It's going to be a tough war.

The Bright-Lights understand the Half-Lits love their shroom juice, but they're praying that their desire for this juice, won't outweigh the need to win the "Fight for Right." They know the jolly-good Half-Lits just want to have fun and they truly enjoy their peaceful life in Happy Hollow. They don't want any trouble and they really don't want to get involved. The Bright-Lights understand that having fun is important, but there comes a time when it's more important to stand up and fight for what's good and what's right. You can't always bury your head in a bottle of juice and avoid doing the hard stuff. There's a time and a place for everything. All of the jolly-good gals understand this principle. Perhaps they will persuade their fellas to join the Bright-Lights, but time is running out.

With their Heart-Lights now in full-glow, the Bright-Lights are hoping that they have enough *Power of Light from Evermore* to defeat the Dark Side. Also, Holy-Hocks and Hydrangel have their wings necklaces, and they will use them to call on other powers of Evermore, if need be. The Tribes and critters gather in a large circle, known as a war circle. Princess Mortania and Chief Two-Feathers are standing in the center, reading their battle plans. The Bright-Light Tribes are fully armed and ready, and they are still waiting for the Half-Lits.

The Bright-Lights *must* continue to protect all that is still good in this beautiful forest. They hope the fighting won't move into the Dale of Derby, but they know what the black-hearted Dragon and his Skanksters have planned. They have battled his hatred and rage for ages.

Peace, hope, love, and joy will always win over hatred, jealousy, and pride. But it takes a little faith, with a flicker of hope and then a whole lot of action. The Bright-Lights had been losing *Faith and Hope* over the ages, due to the endless struggles they had faced every day. They had grown weak and weary from constant battles with the dark side. Over time, their Heart-Light glows had grown dim. They had lost good friends and many neighbors to the dark side. Some had been taken out, some had crossed over to the dark side, and some had simply given up hope. The Bright-Lights Tribe might be smaller in numbers now, but with the return of Holy-Hocks and Hydrangel and their wings necklaces, the power of *hope and faith* has returned.

Holy-Hocks and Hydrangel had been able to find some sense of peace, love, and joy, in Darcy's garden, yet their hearts had been losing hope for the forest. That is, until the visit from Lord Ganador. By connecting to him again, he helped their hearts remember that there is

A Bright-light Battle-camp Meeting

always enough good to outweigh the bad. You just have to look for it. Now, with their Heart-Lights beaming brightly again, their faith in good over evil has been restored. They are ready and willing to fight the good fight. Together, side by side, the Bright-Lights *believe,* they have enough power to win.

The Half-Lits Cast Their Votes

The Half-Lits had been listening to the forest chatter about the war, but they hadn't decided to join the Bright-Lights. They're not fearless warriors, like the others, and they hate fighting. Their jolly-good natures, and "happy go lucky" attitudes make them want to avoid anything dark or negative. They always prefer to look on the bright side of things. Perhaps they could provide a little encouragement, and even some comic relief for the tribes, especially if they get weary and discouraged. Fighting the dark side is serious business, so maybe a little merrymaking could bring relief to the Bright-Lights and rejuvenate their courage and strength. The Half-Lits know that war isn't fun, so they will have to be serious, and stay out of the shroom juice.

The Half-Lits have planned a meeting at the Happy Hollow Pub, to decide if they should join their Bright-Light friends in this "Fight for Right." The Half-Lits understand right from wrong, but they just want to be sure that all of them agree. A vote is required, before any decision can be made. It's a good thing that there are only twenty of the Half-Lits, otherwise the counting could take forever and they must make their decision, asap.

They *could* stand up straight and strong, that is, with a little help from their crooked sticks. They *could* prepare to defend their wonderful forest home and all the marvel that is within it. It *would* be an honor to protect the Bright-Lights and *should* they decide to join them, they *would* do all they *could,* to be rid of the dark things, once and for all. They know the consequences of *"coulda, shoulda, and woulda."* They sure wouldn't want the same *"case of regrets"* sickness their friend Boozle suffers with.

The Half-Lits only weapons are their crooked sticks, pocket knives, and a few red, or green handled shovels; meager weapons at best. But there *is* the shroom juice, and that could be used against the Darkled Tribe. It would make a pretty powerful weapon, if used correctly.

Earlier, when Boozle had heard the trumpet's warning blast, he pulled himself out of bed, and got dressed. He left his house for the first time since he had lost his wife, Drizzle. He walked over to Dorf's house and he knocked on the door. No answer. Then, he headed over to Uncle Harry's house and knocked. No answer there either. Boozle then walked on over to the Happy Hollow Pub. He found all of his friends gathered together, most of them were sitting at a large table. Everyone was there and they were all delighted to see Boozle. It had been a long time.

Dorf hugged his friend Boozle. Together, they sat down with Harry Q. Bindlestick and his four brothers, and all the rest of the jolly-good fellas and gals.

The votes were cast and counted and it was unanimous. They *would* join the Bright-Lights in the "Fight for Right."

Harry Q.'s wife, Geezle, and the gals had prepared meals for the fellas. Knowing how much the fellas love to eat, they served them the Saturday Night Special of canned tomato soup, and grilled cheese sandwiches. They wouldn't allow them any of the shroom juice, not *before or during,* this battle. Boozle already knew how costly that could be. Instead, they drank the cool and clean water from the Living Waters Stream. They needed the good energy this water would provide.

With Boozle by his side, Dorf, the present Commander, assembled all the Half-Lits and their weapons. Together, they marched to the Bright-Light Battle-Camp meeting. A few of the gals stayed behind to pack the food and shroom juice, which they will deliver later. The pudgy fellas will need food for their bellies, and the shroom juice for its magic. The gals had sent the fellas off with flasks full of living water, but no shroom juice.

The jolly-good Half-Lits are a little bit late to the Battle Camp Meeting but, "Better Late than Never."

A Bright-light Battle-camp Meeting

Princess Mortania and Chief Two-Feathers are happy to see this dandy troupe of short, round-bellied, jolly-good fellas and gals. The Bright-Lights thank them for joining them. Dorf, Boozle, Harry Q and his 4-brothers, step up to the Princess and Chief Two-Feathers, and try to bow. Unfortunately, their round bellies wouldn't bend enough to bow, and they started stumbling and rolling all over each other. They quickly grabbed their crooked sticks and stood up straight. Everyone started giggling. The rest of the gals arrived with the food and shroom juice, and stood behind their fellas.

Princess Mortania shot her magic arrow from her three-stringed bow. This arrow flew over each of the jolly-goods and tapped their shoulders, one at a time. Then the arrow flew up and waved over the whole tribe of Half-Lits. Princess Mortania proclaimed, "You are now members of the Bright-Lights Tribe." It was official. Mortania asked the fellas for their beautiful crooked sticks. The fellas laid their sticks at the feet of Princess Mortania and Two-Feathers. The Half-Lits weren't sure what was going to happen to their precious crooked sticks, so they waited and watched.

Chief Two-Feathers took his half-feather out of the pouch on his neck. He waved it over each crooked stick, while chanting in an unfamiliar language. The crooked sticks started to glow and vibrate, then they stood straight up. It was awesome to watch. Gold Dust, fell from the sky and landed on every one of the Bright-Lights.

Princess Mortania picked up the glowing crooked sticks and she handed them back to their owners. She gave the Half-Lits tribe her blessing. As she waved her arrow over the whole pudgy lot of jolly-good fellas and gals, she donned them with a new tribal name, the Bright-Side Tribe.

All the other Bright-Lights cheered and rushed over to welcome each of the jolly-good fellas, and gals. They thanked them for joining them in the "Fight for Right." The Bright-Sides were overwhelmed and humbled. They felt blessed and honored. In fact, they started to celebrate, but Harry Q. Bindlestick shouted, "Stop!" He reminded them that a very significant war was to start soon and they must stay alert, and prepare for action. This was not the time to party.

The Bright-Side Tribe is an honorable new name and well-suited for this jolly-good group who always look on the bright side of things.

The war will begin soon.

. . . . Gold Dust Is Still Falling. . . . .

Chapter 13

Home at Last

After the Bright-Sides (formerly Half-Lits) joined the Bright-Lights, Princess Mortania got her tribes organized. She called up Twinx and Taloop, the male Heart-Lights, who had been hiding in Darcy's garden earlier. She asked them to take Clover and Annabelle back home to Darcy's. She asked them to stay and guard Darcy's garden and critters. She asked Clover to resume her prowling mission and rid the village of as many Dim-Lits and Skanksters as she could. Clover agreed, and said she would get her friends from the Cod-Swallop Dump to help her.

Holy-Hocks and Hydrangel flittered up to the Princess. They were concerned, because it was really late and extremely dark. They wanted to send Annabelle, Clover, Twinx, and Taloop back home *undercover*, to keep them safe. Mortania agreed.

Holy-Hocks and Hydrangel would tap their wings necklaces, and put the "Cloaking Powers" into effect. They had been studying the little book of instructions, so they know which Powers of Evermore to call on for each circumstance. The fairies tapped their wings necklaces and *Poof*, Twinx, Taloop, Annabelle, and Clover disappeared in a second.

The Bright-Lights watch as paw-print indentations, travel along the mossy forest floor. No one could see who was making them and that was all good, but it could be a little tricky if a Skankster happened to see the mossy movements and paw tracks. They will be careful to keep their tracks anonymous.

Clover keeps her eyes wide open. She will warn them, if she spots a Skankster and she will brush their tracks away with her tail to keep them safe. She won't let them down this time. She will stay close beside them all the way. They *believe* the Cloaking Powers will get them home safe, and they did. The Cloaking Powers worked perfectly. That's the way it works when the Powers of Evermore are called upon. No mistakes, no fuss and no fear. All it takes is a little *faith*.

The foursome made it to Darcy's garden. What a day and what a night it had been!

Darcy had been upset and worried all night. She wondered if she'd ever see her precious Annabelle again. Darcy, her mum and her aunt hadn't slept all night. It's 5 am on Saturday morning and almost daylight. Exhausted, the *worriments* hit Darcy hard.

Annabelle had never been away from home before. Darcy had thought that as long as Clover was with her, she'd be OK. All night long she had paced the floor, checking and checking again, but no pup, and no kitty. It's a good thing that nobody had seen Clover, when she *had* returned home earlier last night, *without* Annabelle. They would have been terribly upset to find out that Clover had left Annabelle, all alone in the woods.

Suddenly, there's a scratching and soft whining at the back door. It's Annabelle, and she wants in. As Darcy opens the door to let her pup in, she is overwhelmed with shock at what she sees. Annabelle looks terrible.

Something is definitely wrong with her pup. Annabelle's beautiful golden-brown eyes are all cloudy and milky-white. How can this be? She's not old enough for cataracts. She's not even a whole year old. Only old dogs and old folks get cloudy eyes. What's wrong with Annabelle's

Home At Last

leg? The poor pup is limping and there's a scar on her back leg. Little Annabelle is so happy to see Darcy that she jumps up on her, and practically knocks the girl over. Darcy sits on the floor and hugs her pup. She is overcome with mixed up feelings.

Darcy is happy to have Annabelle home, and yet at the same time she feels sad that her beautiful pup has come back blind and limping. How can she feel happy and sad at the same time? One feeling will override the other, eventually. Right now, the sad feeling is winning and stealing the joy Darcy first felt when her beloved Annabelle had returned.

Darcy stands and then picks Annabelle up and hugs her tight. She lets her tears fall into the pup's soft fur. She kisses the top of her little dog's head, and whispers into her soft, floppy ears. Darcy tells Annabelle, over and over, how much she loves her and how she had missed her. The pup responds with warm, wet puppy-dog-kisses. Then she "dog-talks" back to Darcy in soft "whimper-whines." Eventually, Darcy puts Annabelle down and gives her fresh food and water. Annabelle scarfs down every bit of the food, and laps up all the water in a flash. She was starving.

Darcy feels a terrible sense of guilt, which is unfamiliar to her. She wonders about the decision she made earlier. She was concerned about sending Holy-Hocks and Hydrangel back home to the woods, in the dark. The royal tea party had ended late and then there was the crash. It had turned too dark to let the fairies travel back to the woods all alone.

Darcy learns that some decisions we make, don't always turn out the way we think, or hope they will. She had thought it was a good decision to let Annabelle and Clover escort the two fairies home.

If-onlys rattled in Darcy's head. *If only* the party had ended sooner. *If only* the crash hadn't happened. *If only* it hadn't turned dark. *If only* the fairies had stayed and spent the night. *If only* she hadn't sent Annabelle out into the night.

But the party had ended when it did, and the crash had happened when it did. The day's light had disappeared, and the fairies wanted to go home to the woods and sleep in their own beds.

Darcy had thought it was a good idea to let the fairies ride on top of Annabelle. What had she been thinking? The guilt rises and she begins to question everything. Hadn't she thought that sending Clover along would keep them safe? Wouldn't Clover protect Annabelle, Holy-Hocks and Hydrangel? What had happened out there in the woods? What about Holy-Hocks and Hydrangel? Did they make it home safe?

Worry, worry, Darcy had too many questions and too many *what-ifs?* and *if-onlys*. Her head is pounding. At such a young age, Darcy learns about *guilt* and *regret*. Not all decisions are guaranteed to have either a good or a bad result.

Darcy cries, "I never should have let Annabelle go to the woods in the dark night. I should have made the fairies stay here." Exhausted, she bursts into uncontrollable sobs. She tells her mum, and Aunt Jenny, that she'll never be able to forgive herself.

Her aunt and mother try to comfort her. They tell Darcy that it had been a very good idea at the time, and there was no way to know that Annabelle would be hurt. Her aunt said gently, "We do the best we can, with what we know at the time, and hopefully we make the right decisions. However, sometimes things just happen that we can't foresee or control." She assures Darcy that it *was* a good decision to let Annabelle and Clover take Holy-Hocks and Hydrangel back home, in the dark.

Darcy listens to her aunt, but she still feels sad for Annabelle. She is learning how the powers of *guilt, regret, what ifs,* and *if onlys,* can overwhelm the tender heart of a child. Guilt and regret are unfamiliar to her. She understood abandonment and rejection, but these other feelings are a whole new experience.

Darcy has one more question bothering her. Wasn't sending Clover with them a good thing? She's having mixed feelings about that idea as well. Aunt Jenny tells her, "Clover is a good look-out and she might see danger and be able to protect them. But remember, Clover is still just a cat and that's that. Even Clover can't control everything, and maybe Clover didn't even see what happened to Annabelle. Speaking of Clover, where the heck is that cat, anyway?"

Home At Last

Clover had just finished settling Twinx and Taloop into the garden. She had given them instructions to stay alert, and to let her know if they spotted an icky menacer. She warned them to be careful, and then she turned and headed into the house through the open bedroom window.

Clover hears the commotion in the kitchen and she saunters in to see what it's all about. As she enters the kitchen, she sees Darcy crying over the pup and she feels bad for the little girl. She knows how much Annabelle means to everyone, especially Darcy. Clover is truly sorry she left the pup in the woods and even sorrier that Annabelle had been hurt.

Clover actually has a soft spot in her heart for these humans, and her doggie companion. She is *grateful* to share her life with all of them.

Time and experience changes all things, including folks and critters.

Clover walks over to her favorite human, Aunt Jenny, and rubs against Jenny's leg, purring loudly. Then she meows, "Hungry cat here!" Jenny gets the message and she fixes her cat a big plate of canned tuna and a bowl of warm milk. Clover had trained her human very well and she is a contented cat right now.

Annabelle and Clover are happy to be home safe, well fed, and well loved. Darcy keeps hugging her pup and soon her emotions settle down.

Chapter 14

The Cat from Cod-Swallop

Aunt Jenny has always loved the curious ways of cats, and Clover is extremely curious. Aunt Jenny and Clover spend a lot of time together; most evenings, Clover sleeps on Jenny's lap. For Aunt Jenny, petting her cat's silky fur and listening to her soft purrs has already softened her grief. When Aunt Jenny's husband, Edward, had passed, Ruthie invited Aunt Jenny to come and live with her and Darcy. This was about the same time that Darcy's father had left, leaving her and her mother abandoned and all alone. Since Edward was Ruthie's brother, she felt it was the right thing to do. So, Aunt Jenny came to live with Ruthie and Darcy; and it has been a blessing for all of them.

To help Aunt Jenny through her grief, Ruthie brought home a stray kitten, which had been a nuisance to the neighbors. She didn't want the kitten to be taken to the dump. Lots of folks like to take stray animals, or even pets they simply don't want anymore, to the dump. Very sad, but very true.

Ruthie didn't know this, but Clover had actually been thriving at the dump for a couple of months before Ruthie had taken her in. The un-wanted kitty had been dropped off at the dump by the dust cart,

The Cat From Cod-swallop

which picks up trash and garbage in several of the neighboring villages. The driver of the dust cart hauls the garbage to the Waste Management Refuse Center, also known as the dump. It is located in Cod-Swallop, just a few miles northeast of the Bo-Peeps.

Every now and then, the driver of the dust cart, "Haulin' Hank," makes a little cash on the side when he takes an unwanted pup or kitty to the dump...pitiful.

Before Ruthie had ever taken the kitty in, Clover's curiosity had caused her to wander away from the dump and she ended up in the Dale of Derby. She had been stalking a "Skankster" and it led her right into the Dale.

Clover used to catch and release Skanksters because they tasted horrible, and she could never eat one. She knows just how bad these Skanksters are; she had observed some of their terrible deeds. Therefore, when Clover came to live with Aunt Jenny, she made it her mission to rid her new domain, the Dale of Derby, of their presence. This is *her* territory now!

The Buzzard's Palace

Whenever Clover catches Skanksters, she does what she must to get rid of them. Sometimes she might have to leave their yucky carcasses for the buzzards to pick up themselves, but only when she's too busy and doesn't have time to carry them off to the dump.

Clover, being the clever negotiator that she is, has a splendid working relationship with the Cod-Swallop Buzzards and her friends from the Refuse Center, the Dump Dogs and Trash Cats.

Most of the time, these friends will carry the dead Skankster carcasses to Cod-Swallop and drop them off onto the front deck of the Buzzard's Palace. The front deck, called "For the Birds," is an outdoor, fine dining and lounge area just for the buzzards. These big birds enjoy the tasty Skankster carcasses and usually stay out of the Dale, waiting for their meals to be delivered. Imagine that, a palace and free meal delivery, just for a bunch of dirty birds. What's next?

The buzzards eat the stinky carcasses, so the Cod-Swallop Dump doesn't stink as bad as it used to.

The Cat From Cod-swallop

With help from her Dump Dogs and Trash Cats friends, Clover is keeping the carcasses and the buzzards out of the Dale so it doesn't smell. The buzzards hang out at the dump instead of in the Dale. Villagers reward Clover and her friends with canned tuna and fresh milk: it's a win-win situation for all.

Aunt Jenny had taken a liking to this kitty right away, and Clover accepted Aunt Jenny because she gave Clover canned tuna and fresh, warm milk every day. As a kitten, Clover had been seen eating fresh clover out in Marion's Meadow—hence the name. No one knew why the cat ate clover.

Today, after returning home, Clover is feeling something new in her heart. It seems with all her pride and independence, Clover realizes just how much these humans and her dog friend Annabelle mean to her, and how much she depends on them. She is grateful to be a part of this loving family. She will fiercely protect each of them, and she will try not take them for granted anymore.

Pets are so good for us humans for many reasons. They bring their own special gifts to those of us who have the privilege of sharing life with them. They are good medicine for lots of ailments. They bring us joy when we are sad. They give us comfort when we grieve. They fill our empty hearts when we are lonesome. They are forgiving when we are angry. They are faithful and they love us unconditionally, just like God does. Cats and dogs are God's special gifts to us. They are loyal friends with fur; we all need our fur-friends.

The ladies had spent a sleepless night worrying about their two precious pets. Aunt Jenny was relieved to have Clover home and as soon as she placed the plate of canned tuna on the floor, the cat gave Aunt Jenny a quick kiss. *Amazing*, Jenny thought. It's a rare honor to be kissed by any cat, let alone by Clover.

Aunt Jenny thinks to herself, "What a difference a day makes."

While tending to Annabelle, the pup acts as if she wants to play. Darcy throws the pup's favorite ball. Although Annabelle can't see, she can hear and smell; and within seconds, she locates exactly where the ball lands. She picks it up with her teeth, carries it back to Darcy, and drops it right in front of the girl's feet. Darcy claps her hands, praises the pup, and scratches the top of her head. Then she tosses the ball even further and tells Annabelle to go fetch. Once again, without a moment's hesitation, this amazing, little dog retrieves her ball and brings it right back to Darcy.

Joy has once again returned; it has replaced the momentary sadness in Darcy's heart. It seems as if Annabelle isn't bothered by her blindness at all. Dogs have amazing senses, far greater than humans. Although Annabelle has lost her sight, her hearing and smelling senses have become much sharper. Dogs don't dwell on their shortcomings either, like some humans tend to do. Dogs live in the moment.

The little game of catch turns into a beautiful bonding moment for Darcy and her dog. It's a moment in time when they have connected to each other in a way that some humans will never understand. Though she is blind and walks with a limp, Annabelle is still one happy puppy, and Darcy is one happy, little girl. The love Darcy is sharing with Annabelle right now, in this precious moment in time, is a very unique kind of love. It's a beautiful love, which Darcy will carry in her heart's memories for the rest of her life. The bond between a human's spirit and a sensitive dog's spirit is unexplainable.

Darcy and Annabelle continue playing catch, filling their home with love, laughter, and happy, little puppy barks. After the game of catch, everyone decides that a good nap is in order, even though it is morning. It is very early Saturday morning, so they can sleep in. There is plenty of time for a good sleep. Last night Pastor Charles had asked the villagers to meet him at the Good Church, 6 pm Saturday, for a special prayer meeting.

Clover settles herself on Aunt Jenny's lap, and the two doze off in the chair. Ruthie gets into her bed and falls into a deep sleep. Darcy carries Annabelle upstairs to her bedroom and gently lays her on the bed, right next to her. The two are happy to snuggle. Exhausted, they fall fast asleep. Their home fills with the peaceful sounds of snoring and all is right in Darcy's wonderful world.

As Darcy drifts off to sleep, she begins dreaming of what might have happened to Annabelle in the woods last night. While asleep, her dream becomes more and more like a vision of things to come—so much so that when she finally awakens, Darcy's reality and dream has merged into her consciousness.

Chapter 15

Powers from Evermore

Princess Mortania sounds her final trumpet warning, announcing the war. All vulnerable woodland critters are tucked into their safety zones. The stronger critters—the ones who are able to fight—are ready to help the Bright-Lights.

With their wings necklaces, Holy-Hocks and Hydrangel have covered each of the Heart-Light Fairies with the Enchanting Powers of Evermore. Several of them have been cloaked; others were given unique war powers, enabling them to fight the good fight with special protection.

Princess Mortania and Chief Two-Feathers have studied their battle plans. They are fully armed and ready to battle the evil forces. Several of the Moratores had been lost in previous battles, so Mortania and Two-Feathers are grateful to have Holy-Hocks and Hydrangel with their wings necklaces.

The jolly-good, Bright-Side fellas have been fed by their jolly-good gals. The wings necklaces had been used to add powers from Evermore to their simple weapons. The red or green handled shovels, little pocket knives, crooked sticks, and "shroom" juice have been turned into weapons of mass destruction.

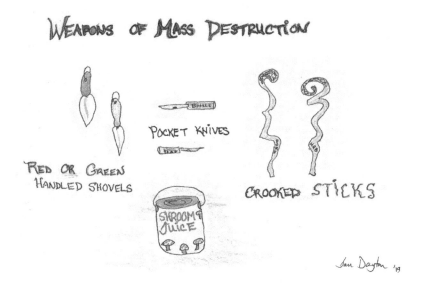

The Bright-Sides have finished filling Jack-in-the-Pulpit flowers with the shroom juice. Skanksters and Dim-Lits always drink rain waters that gather in the plant's trumpet-shaped flowers. Let's see what happens to these icky creeps once they drink the powered-up shroom juice.

Hopefully, the Dim-Lits and Skanksters will be defeated without any major casualties to any of the Bright-Lights. Every one of the Dim-Lit Muddlers had decided to stand with the evil Skanksters. They had gathered their huge arsenal of muddy weapons, including the favored mud-pies, mud-balls, and mud-wumps. They are prepared, mudded up, and ready for war. The Darkled Tribe had been practicing their shape-shifting powers and other skills, and they are convinced they are going to win this war.

Marskank has given his orders to Flat Fangle and to Gog-Mantle as well. He feels it wise to have the two commanders, in case one of them fails. He had lost confidence in Fangle, ever since the Tractor Tire Transformation. The Darkled Dragon will direct each commander from his Skanky Pond post. Gog-Mantle will head up the battle, while Flat Fangle runs reports back and forth to Marskank.

    The Skanky Pond has started to boil; it is bubbling and gurgling. A grey cloud of putrid air is leaching out of the swamp, while a deep, growling howl travels through the woods and the forest ground trembles.

Chapter 16

The Quietude

It's Saturday morning, a brand-new day. Sun streaks beam through the window, casting glittery reflections on the bedroom wall. Darcy wakes up groggy from a strange dream. She hadn't slept at all the night before; she'd gone to bed just before dawn. Confused, Darcy wonders what time it is and what day it is. She rubs her eyes and yawns. She looks to the foot of her bed and Annabelle isn't there. She crawls out of bed and calls her dog. Annabelle doesn't respond.

It's very still and quiet in her house—way too quiet. Darcy wonders if everyone is still sleeping. Maybe Annabelle went downstairs to wake up someone to let her outside to go potty. Darcy quietly walks down the staircase and half-way down, she sees Aunt Jenny sound asleep in her chair, with Clover still on her lap. Her mother's bedroom door is closed, which probably means Ruthie is still sleeping. It had been a long night and no one had gone to bed before dawn. Darcy looks at the clock on the living room mantle; it is 10 am. This means she only got about four hours of sleep; no wonder she's so fog-headed. She goes into the kitchen, hoping to find Annabelle, but the pup is nowhere in sight. After all the worriment last night, Darcy tries to stay calm and find her pup. She looks all through the kitchen, including the butler's pantry. She checks the dining room and then she walks back into the living room.

She doesn't want to wake Aunt Jenny or Clover. Too late; the cat is aware of her presence, and she looks up at Darcy. She stretches, yawns, and jumps down from Aunt Jenny's lap. She rubs against Darcy, hoping the girl will get her some tuna and fresh milk. As Darcy reaches down to pet the cat, Clover lets out a "meow." That's all it takes to wake up Aunt Jenny. She apologizes to her aunt, but Aunt Jenny is ready to get up anyway and get dressed. She asks Darcy where Annabelle is, and Darcy just shrugged her shoulders. Aunt Jenny thinks she ought to help Darcy look for her dog, as she knows how the girl worries.

It's way too quiet throughout the big house; there isn't any noise outside either. This is highly unusual for this late in the morning, especially on a Saturday. Aunt Jenny opens the windows to let the fresh air in and peek outside. There's no breeze, and not even a bird chirps. Usually by this time of morning, you hear bird-song, bees buzzing, and leaves rustling in the breezes. But not today. There's an eerie and quiet hush over the entire village. Nobody is out and about for an early morning stroll, or even for a bicycle ride. Aunt Jenny calls it a quietude, a "calm before a storm." It is peaceful, but almost in a forewarning way.

All of a sudden, a dog whimper comes from upstairs. Darcy looks up and there is Annabelle sitting at the top of the stairs, thumping her tail on the wood floor. Darcy calls her, and she limps slowly down the stairs, heading to the back door. She has to go potty. Annabelle isn't limping too bad, and it's hard to tell that she is blind. Darcy runs outside, still in her pajamas, after the pup. As far as Darcy can tell, it looks as if Annabelle is doing much better. In fact, after she has gone potty, the pup sniffs around and now it seems she wants to play.

Darcy calls her pup, "Annabelle, come." The dog responds right away, limps over to Darcy, and sits down in front of her. Her eyes are not quite as cloudy as they were. Darcy feels Annabelle's back leg and there is a scar and a bump, but no evidence of any pain. Maybe the dog

The Quietude

would heal after a while and Darcy prays that she will be able to see again, someday.

She takes Annabelle back inside and feeds her. Her mother is up now, fixing breakfast.

Darcy begins talking to her mum. She asks her mother if she thought that Annabelle would get better over time. Ruthie thought carefully for a moment and said this, "I believe her leg might heal a little more over time, but she might be blind the rest of her life and limp. She will still be your friend, and she will love you and always play with you, even if she stays blind. Please don't treat Annabelle as if she is handicapped. She doesn't think she is. Just treat her like you always have." Darcy nods in agreement.

The quietude continues, both inside the house and outside. Still, no bird-song, no villagers milling about, and no breezes: just stillness and silence. She asks her mum and aunt, "Why is it so quiet?" The two women stop and look at each other. They tell her that maybe it is just "one of those days." Confused and still groggy, Darcy eats her breakfast, then goes upstairs to dress. In a bit, she comes back down to the kitchen.

Clover laps up the last drop of her milk and sits down to clean herself. Annabelle finishes her meal, and finds her favorite ball and drops it in front of Darcy. She does her cute, little puppy circles and jumps up and down. She is ready to play catch, so Darcy takes her out to the garden and plays ball with her. After a few tosses and fetches, the pup tires and lays down in the grass. It's now 11 am on this beautiful, sunny Saturday morning, but it is still too quiet, until the knock on the garden gate. It's Robin, Darcy's new best friend.

Robin and his folks had moved to the Dale about a year ago. In school, Robin and Darcy took a quick liking to each other and soon became *besties* (thanks to Holy-Hocks and Hydrangel). Robin loves to come over and play with Annabelle and Clover. He doesn't have any pets, but he has always wanted a puppy. His dad keeps promising him, "someday." He loves hearing Darcy's stories and eating scones. Even though he is not a big fan of drinking tea from a fancy teacup, he pretends to enjoy it because he likes hanging out with Darcy.

Darcy and Robin stay in the garden for a bit, playing with Annabelle and Clover. Darcy can hardly wait to tell him about her dream. He brings up the strange quiet, which was becoming annoyingly curious. "Where are all the birds and other critters? Why is the air so still, and why aren't people out and about?" he asks.

They sit and chat all about the quietude thing for a bit, and then they both decide there are more exciting things they could talk about. He wants to hear all about her dream, but he really wants to take a walk to the duck pond, and maybe go into the forest and collect pine cones.

Darcy thinks a walk will be nice, and Robin says, "You can tell me all about your dream while we walk in the woods." *Splendid idea*, Darcy thought, but she isn't going to take Annabelle or Clover into the woods. When Robin asks why not, she tells him she will explain it all when she tells him about her dream. Darcy puts Annabelle and Clover back inside the house and grabs her sweater, and she and Robin go for their walk.

They cross Marion's Meadow and stop at the duck pond, but the ducks aren't there, so they head toward the woods. They walk over the foot bridge and step into the woods, staying on the soft, mossy path. It's eerily quiet in the forest and a sense of dread comes over Darcy, but she tries to ignore it. They continue walking and start gathering up pine cones.

Darcy begins telling Robin about her dream. She is afraid that Holy-Hocks and Hydrangel are in danger because of the evil dragon, Marskank, and his gang of Skanksters living in Skanky Pond. She says they hate everything that is good, and they are planning to destroy the Stickety Wicket Woods, the Bright-Lights Fairies, the forest folks, and even the Prince of Evermore. She tells him they want to take over the Dale of Derby and beyond. Already exhausted from lack of sleep, Darcy is becoming confused and frightened. To her, the dream seems too real.

She continues, but as she starts to tell Robin about the Gala Coach and horses crashing into the deep hole (that had mysteriously opened

The Quietude

up), he stops her. "Darcy, that part wasn't a dream. I was there with my parents and the crowd of village folks watching, right after it happened." Darcy sits down on the ground and shakes. Robin sits next to her. He can see she's upset.

Darcy begins to cry. She tells Robin that she had sent Annabelle and Clover to take Holy-Hocks and Hydrangel back to the woods after the crash, because it was too dark for them to go alone. Clover and Annabelle had been in the woods all night and when they finally came home, Annabelle was blind and limping. She said, "That's why I left her and Clover back at the house." He understands.

Then Darcy remembers about the angel wings necklaces the prince had given Holy-Hocks and Hydrangel so they could call down the powers of Evermore. As she's telling Robin about them, she remembers her own necklace and reaches for it, but it's gone. She must find it before it gets into the wrong hands. He promises to help her.

Then she tells Robin the part of her dream where she had envisioned a war between evil forces and all that is true and good.

All of a sudden, she and Robin hear something awful.

Right up until that moment, there hadn't been a sound of any kind. What they just heard ran chills down their spines, and they decided it might be best to turn around and go back. As they leave the forest, a low, growling howl came out of the middle of the swamp. Darcy and Robin start to run. They run all the way back to the safety of Darcy's garden.

Robin leaves Darcy's and heads home, and she goes into her house. She is tired, confused, and feeling sick. She decides to go to bed early tonight. She won't go to the church meeting tonight with Aunt Jenny and her mother. She calls Annabelle, and together they go upstairs and stay in her room. Darcy wonders how she could have lost her wings necklace. She can't stop thinking about it and, after searching, it's not in her room.

She is glad she had told Robin about her dream, but since he hadn't attended the royal tea party, she doesn't think he believes her about the wings necklaces. She knows he believes the part about the crash, because he and his parents had heard the commotion and had joined the others to see what had happened.

Robin hadn't paid attention to rumors of Bright-Light Fairies and little folks living in the Stickety Wicket Woods. He does, however, find the stories about an evil dragon and his Skankster Gang very intriguing.

Robin knows Darcy is a great storyteller, so he isn't sure if he believes everything she has just told him. As he had been listening to her, he kept wondering if she was making it up, until she got to the part about the crash. He knows that part is true because he had seen it for himself. He doesn't know if she has a wings necklace or not, but he had promised to help her look for it. He knew something strange was going on with that *quietude* thing, but a war in the woods between fairies, little folks, and evil monsters, really? But, then again, there was that scary growl.

Robin definitely would be going with his parents to the meeting at the Good Church tonight at 6 pm. His folks had said it would be important. He is curious.

By the end of the day, Darcy realizes that what she thought was a dream was actually reality mixed with something else; something she didn't understand. Was it a premonition, or perhaps a vision? If only she can find her wings necklace, she will have a better understanding.

Tomorrow will be another day, and right now, Darcy is content to snuggle with Annabelle.

Chapter 17

Wings

Darcy's alarm clock wakes her up. It's 8 am, Sunday morning. She heads downstairs where her mum and Aunt Jenny are preparing breakfast. Clover is lapping her milk, and Annabelle is just finishing her meal. As soon as the pup hears Darcy, she limps over to the girl for a pet.

Yesterday, Darcy and Robin had gone for a walk in the Stickety Wicket Woods. It had been way too quiet in the forest, until the growling howl; the howl that made them run all the way back to Darcy's garden.

Darcy asks her mum if she has seen her wings necklace. Ruthie tells her daughter no, but she probably has misplaced it with all the commotion going on. Darcy can't believe it. She *has* to find it. Maybe Aunt Jenny has seen it.

Aunt Jenny tells Darcy that when she came downstairs around 10 am yesterday morning (Saturday), she was pretty groggy. She could have lost it in the garden outside, or in the woods where she and Robin had walked.

Sitting at the kitchen table, petting Annabelle, Darcy feels a twinge of sadness enter her heart. Sensing this sadness, Annabelle gets her ball and drops it at Darcy's feet. Immediately, the sadness leaves and she is happy to play with Annabelle.

After breakfast, Ruthie reminds Darcy to go upstairs and get ready for church. Darcy and Annabelle climb the stairs together, and soon Darcy is dressed and ready to go. There is no Sunday School class this morning. Pastor Charles has decided to have everyone meet in the sanctuary for a special meeting, instead of his usual sermon. He has much to say about all the events that had taken place Friday, after the royal tea party.

At 11 am, the church bell rings, and everyone takes their seats in the sanctuary. Pastor Charles steps up to the pulpit and asks the folks to bow their heads. He says a long prayer of gratitude and then begins talking.

He tells the folks about a terrible commotion that had taken place in the Stickety Wicket Woods late Friday night and well into Saturday. He says he's not sure what happened, after Lord Ganador had left the Dale of Derby.

He feels certain that a war had taken place in the woods. A war between good and evil; a "Fight for Right." He doesn't know what happened to the forest folks, the critters, Holy-Hocks and Hydrangel, and the Bright-Lights. He mentions the mysterious *quietude* that went on all day Saturday. He said it was like the "calm before a storm," just as Aunt Jenny had said. Then he asks the folks, "Could it have been the calm *after* the storm?" He's not sure, and neither are the folks.

He thanks all who had attended the 6 pm prayer meeting last night. Everyone had stayed for more than an hour praying for protection.

Pastor Charles believes that because of their prayers, a *hedge of protection* has been placed around the Dale, and that is why no one has been hurt. He also believes that the guardians had protected the Stickety Wicket Woods, and all the woodland critters, as best as they could. He reminds them that Holy-Hocks and Hydrangel had been given the wings necklaces for a *divine* purpose. He wonders if troops from Evermore might have been called down to rescue the Bright-Lights from the dragon and his evil menacers. He's not certain, but he is hopeful.

Wings

The folks of the faith agree with him, and they understand that the only way to overcome evil is with the powers from Evermore. Only time will tell what really happened.

Darcy thought about all this. She is concerned for Holy-Hocks and Hydrangel, and wonders what might have happened to her precious fairy friends. She wants to go to her garden and fix tea and scones, and wait to see if they'll show up. When church is over, that's exactly what she will do. The church meeting ends. Robin walks over to Darcy and they chat for a few minutes. Darcy tells him what she is planning to do when she gets home. She invites Robin to come over, and he says he will, right after Sunday dinner with his parents. He believes her.

Robin and Darcy are in the garden, drinking orange mint tea and eating wild-berry scones, waiting for the two fairies to show up. They play ball with Annabelle and Clover until late in the afternoon, when Robin has to go home. Darcy is disappointed that Holy-Hocks and Hydrangel didn't show up; maybe tomorrow.

Before Darcy goes inside, she searches the garden one more time for her wings necklace. She doesn't find it, and it's getting late. Her mother calls her inside.

Soon after supper, Darcy is in her room getting ready for bed. Annabelle is sitting on top of the girl's bed. All of a sudden, a soft, glittery streak of golden light comes streaming through the bedroom window. Darcy walks over to the window to look out and there, on the window sill, sits a gold-wrapped gift box, just like the one she had received from Lord Ganador. She opens it. Inside are three angel wings necklaces, two tiny ones and a larger one. It's her necklace and the ones belonging to Holy-Hocks and Hydrangel. She starts to weep. What does this mean?

A soft beam of golden light brightens and catches her attention. She looks out the window.

She sees what appears to be two, huge, beautiful angels, dressed in shimmery white gowns, standing over her garden. Their glorious wings are spread open, and there's a glowing beam of light surrounding them. She watches in awe as gold dust drops from the sky and spreads golden glitters all over her garden. Then, the angels look directly at Darcy. They smile at her, and quick as a wink, they disappear into the dark night sky.

As soon as she had seen them, Darcy knew in her heart of hearts that Holy-Hocks and Hydrangel had chosen to go back to Evermore to be with Lord Ganador. He must have allowed them to come back and show themselves to Darcy. They had found her necklace and placed it in the gift box on her window sill with their wings necklaces. A sense of peace and comfort washes over the little girl. She knows she is loved in a way she doesn't exactly understand, but her heart is happy and full. She feels safe and protected. She kneels to say her prayers, and then crawls into bed and snuggles up to her beautiful Annabelle.

Holding her angel wings necklace and thinking about Holy-Hocks and Hydrangel, Darcy drifts peacefully off to sleep, knowing that she will see them again, someday.

Coming in Spring/Summer of 2020:

Volume 2: The War in the Stickety Wicket Woods

This war, the "Fight for Right", had been brewing in the ancient forest for a long time. After so many battles, it was time to put an end to the evil menacers. And so, it finally began late one Moon-Lit night.

What happened in the Stickety Wicket Woods between the Bright-Lights and the Darkled Dragon's Skankster Gang? Where are the Guardians, Holy-Hocks and Hydrangel and the rest of the forest folks and woodland critters? What happened to Darcy's wings necklace, after she lost it? Find out what happens to Annabelle and Clover, when they and their friends, dare to venture into the woods to search for their friends, the forest folks and woodland critters.

ACKNOWLEDGMENTS:

I'd like to thank all my wonderful friends for their encouragement, and prayers.

Thank you Joyce, for introducing me to fairy gardens and tea-times. Thank you, Doris and April, (fellow writers) for your encouragement and prayers. Thank you Carol (BFF) for your loyalty, prayers and encouragement. Thanks Carol L, for your help and prayers. Thanks to Dale, Carol and Laura (my special cousins) for inspiring and encouraging me.

I'd like to express my deepest appreciation for the amazing team at Xulon Press/Salem Author Services: Steven, for his endless patience and willingness to help. Toni for her prayers, help and encouragement. Greg for his kindness, patience, and help. Thanks to the editors, and other team members for making this possible.

CPSIA information can be obtained
at www.ICGtesting.com
Printed in the USA
BVHW071455141019
561050BV00003B/252/P